Daniel Wilson

William Nelson

A Memoir

Daniel Wilson

William Nelson
A Memoir

ISBN/EAN: 9783337423513

Printed in Europe, USA, Canada, Australia, Japan

Cover: Foto ©Andreas Hilbeck / pixelio.de

More available books at **www.hansebooks.com**

William   Nelson.

William Nelson

A MEMOIR

BY

SIR DANIEL WILSON, LL.D., F.R.S.E.,
PRESIDENT OF THE UNIVERSITY OF TORONTO.

Printed for Private Circulation.

T. Nelson and Sons, Edinburgh.

1889.

TO

Mrs. William Nelson

THIS

MEMOIR OF HER HUSBAND

IS AFFECTIONATELY DEDICATED BY

HIS OLD FRIEND AND

SCHOOLMATE

FOREWORD.

THE volume here produced for the eye of friends is the memorial of one whose life presented a rare example of simplicity, of thoroughness in working up to a high standard in all that he undertook, and fidelity in his responsible stewardship as a man of wealth and a captain of industry. The friendship between us extended in uninterrupted union, with the maturing estimation of years and experience, from early boyhood till both had passed the assigned limits of threescore years and ten. It would have been easy to swell the volume into the bulky proportions of modern biography: for William Nelson keenly enjoyed the communion of friendship; and his correspondence furnishes many passages calculated to interest others besides those who knew and loved him as a friend. But the aim has been simply to present him "in his habit as he lived;" and thus to preserve for relatives, personal friends, and for his fellow-workers of all ranks, such a picture as may pleasantly recall some reflex of a noble life; and record characteristic traits of one of whom it can be so truly said: "To live in hearts of those we love is not to die."

D. W.

UNIVERSITY OF TORONTO,
September 26, 1889.

CONTENTS.

William Nelson.

CHAPTER I.

INTRODUCTORY.

IN the early years of the present century the Scottish capital retained many features of its ancient aspect still unchanged; but among all the old-world haunts surviving into modern times, the most notable, alike for its picturesque quaintness and its varied associations, was the avenue from the Grassmarket to the upper town. The West Bow, as this thoroughfare was called, derived its name from the ancient bow, or archway, which gave entrance to the little walled city before the civic area was extended by the Flodden wall of 1513. But the archway remained long after that date as the entrance to the upper town—the Temple Bar of Edinburgh—at which the ceremonial welcome of royal and distinguished visitors took place.

The West Bow had accordingly been the scene of

many a royal cavalcade of the Jameses and their queens; as well as of such representative men as Ben Jonson and his brother-poet Drummond of Hawthornden, of Laud, Montrose, Leslie, Cromwell, and Dundee. Among its quaint antique piles were the gabled Temple Lands, St. James's Altar Land, and the timber-fronted lodging of Lord Ruthven, the ruthless leader in the tragedy when Lord Darnley's minions assassinated Rizzio in Queen Mary's chamber at Holyrood. There, too, remained till very recent years the haunted house of the prince of Scottish wizards, Major Weir; and near by the Clockmaker's Land, noted to the last for the ingenious piece of workmanship of Paul Remieu, a Huguenot refugee of the time of Charles II. Nearly opposite was the dwelling of Provost Stewart, where, in the famous '45, he entertained Prince Charles Edward, while Holyrood was for the last time the palace of the Stuarts. The alley which gave access to the old Jacobite provost's dwelling bore in its last days the name of Donaldson's Close; for here was the home of one of Edinburgh's most prosperous typographers, James Donaldson, who bequeathed the fortune won by his craft to found the magnificent hospital which now rivals that of the royal goldsmith of James I.

Such were some of the antique surroundings amid which the subject of the present memoir passed his youth, and which no doubt had their influence in developing an archæological taste, and that reverence for every historical feature of his native city, which bore good fruit in later years. But his more intimate associations were with the singularly picturesque timber-fronted dwelling at the head of the West Bow, with another fine elevation toward the Lawnmarket, which, till 1878, stood unchanged as when the Flodden king rode past on his way to the Borough Moor. A painting of the old house adorned the walls at Salisbury Green in later years; and when at last the venerable structure was demolished, some of its oaken timbers were secured by William Nelson and fashioned into antique furniture for himself and his friends. This picturesque building was the haunt of an old Edinburgh bookseller, the founder of the well-known printing and publishing house of Thomas Nelson and Sons.

Mr. Thomas Nelson, the father of the subject of the present memoir, and the originator of the great publishing firm, recurs to the present writer in the memories of his own early years as a fine example of the old Scottish type of silent, indomitable perseverance and sterling integrity. The traditions of the race are thus set forth in a memorandum in William Nelson's handwriting:—" The Nelsons of our branch resided at Throsk, a few miles east from Stirling, not far from the field of Bannockburn. There was a tradition among us that some of our race lived there at the time the battle was fought, and as a boy I was willing to believe it." There, at any rate, the Nelsons are known to have been for four or five generations; and Thomas Nelson was born at Throsk in 1780. His grandmother had seceded with the Erskines from the National Church; and the spirit of that elder race of Scottish nonconformists was inherited by their children. They joined a congregation of Reformed Presbyterians, or Covenanters, at Stirling; and the boy grew up on his father's farm under all the influences of that earnest, unwavering religious faith, which has so often seemed the fitting complement to the ruggedness of the Scottish character, while it has, in not a few instances, furnished the best preparation for a successful career in business. His father led a retired life on his carse farm, with Stirling sufficiently near to admit of his enjoying the privilege of regular worship with the devout little band of Presbyterian nonconformists there. So little was he affected by the enterprise of younger generations that he could not be persuaded to turn to profitable account a small pottery on the land he occupied. He was content with the humble career of a small farmer. But the monotony of farm-life was varied by long journeys, staff in hand, in which the boy accompanied his father, to attend the great gatherings at the sacramental seasons.

In the persecuting times the devout adherents of the Covenant had been wont to assemble in some secluded glen to enjoy in safety the privileges of the communion service, and their descendants continued the practice in more peaceful times. Under such training the boy reached his sixteenth year, when, after a brief experience as a teacher, some chance report of prosperous adventure in the West Indies tempted the youth with its illusive visions. Bidding his friends and home farewell, his father accompanied him for some miles on the road to Alloa, giving his best counsel and advice to the lad by the way. When they reached the place of parting, his father said to him, " Thomas, my boy, have you ever thought that where you are going you will be far away from the means of grace ? " " No, father," said he, " I never thought of that, and I won't go."

Thus abruptly the scheme was abandoned. They retraced their steps to the old farm, and the boy found employment for a time at Craigend, near Stirling. There he formed the acquaintance of Symington, whose steam-engine was first applied to navigation, and sailed with him in some of the earliest trial-trips on the Carron Water. The pottery which his father had neglected was started on a neighbouring farm, and young Nelson was anxious to get the management of it. But the scheme appears to have been distasteful to his father, whose secret desire probably was that

his boy should follow his own example, and so escape
the world's trials and temptations. But the son's am-
bition aimed at something more advantageous than the
homely career of a lowland farmer; and so, by-and-
by, he betook himself to London, entered the service
of a publishing house there, and began the training
which ultimately begot the great publishing firm that
bears his name.

The young Scottish Covenanter did not forget his
early training, amid the temptations of the great
metropolis. Along with a few other Scotchmen of his
own age, he established a weekly meeting for religious
fellowship; and it is told of one of the little band, who
was employed at the dock-yard, that he forfeited his
situation rather than work on the Sabbath day. But
he had already won the favourable opinion of Lord
Melville, who, on learning of his dismissal, severely re-
buked the officials, and soon after advanced him to a
higher post. From London, Thomas Nelson made his
way to Edinburgh with what little capital his frugality
had enabled him to accumulate, and there he started
his first book-store, stocked chiefly with second-hand
books, but from which ere long he began the issue of
cheap reprints of the "Scots Worthies" and other
popular religious works, in monthly parts. He had to
proceed cautiously in this new venture, for his capital
was small; but he had the courage to shape out a

course of his own. With sagacious foresight he over-
leapt the intermediate stages of publishing and bookselling, and grafted on to the traffic of the mediæval
fairs some of the most modern usages of free trade.
The full results of this bold step are even now only
partially developed, though its ultimate advantages are
beginning to be generally recognized, and to force
themselves on the attention of the great publishing
houses, accustomed hitherto to cater only with small
editions of costly volumes for the libraries of the
wealthy, supplemented in recent years by the expedient
of lending libraries.

The removal of Mr. Thomas Nelson's book-store to
the picturesque tenement at the Bowhead marks the
first progressive step of the young innovator. The
venerable timber - fronted land projected with each
successive story in advance of the lower one, after the
fashion of that obsolete civic architecture in vogue
before Newton had revealed his law of gravitation.
The first story above the paving rested on substantial
oak piers, forming a piazza opening on to the Bow,
within which stood the exposed book - stall of the
primitive trader. Behind this was the stone-vaulted
buith, or shop, as in the old luckenbuiths alongside of
St. Giles's Cathedral. The north façade fronted on the
Lawnmarket, a wide thoroughfare, where at certain
seasons the dealers in linens and woollens set up their

stalls, much after the fashion which the poet Dunbar describes them hampering the High Street before the Flodden wall was built. Already at that early date the printing-press of Walter Chepman, the Scottish Caxton, was at work; and before long the craft had its representatives among the traders' buiths. In a later century Allan Ramsay began his prosperous career as a seller of his own metrical "broadsides;" and Dr. Johnson's father, the respected bookseller and magistrate of the cathedral city of Lichfield, was wont to set up his book-stall on market days in the neighbouring towns.

Here then, at the Bowhead, with its north front to the Lawnmarket, stood within our own recollection the well-stored book-stall, the nucleus and germ of the great Parkside printing establishment, with its hundreds of workmen in every branch of the trade. The busy scene of a market day in the old locality, as it could still be seen sixty-five years ago, is graphically depicted in Turner's view of the High Street, engraved in 1825 for Sir Walter Scott's "Provincial Antiquities." The book-trade, as prosecuted by Mr. Thomas Nelson, depended in no inconsiderable degree on the application of the stereotyping process to the production of cheap editions of popular works of established repute. He was a pioneer in the production of literature for the million; but he catered for the taste of an age very different from our own, in his effort to put standard works, already stamped with the approval of the wise and good, within reach of the peasant and the artisan. " The Pilgrim's Progress " was already an English classic; and with this were issued such works as Baxter's " Saints' Rest," Booth's " Reign of Grace," " MacEwan on the Types," and other works of a like class. To those were by-and-by added Jeremy Taylor, Leighton, Romaine, and Newton, the old Scottish and Puritan divines, and Josephus, all produced by means of stereotype plates, which admitted of a limited issue adapted to the demand of the market. With the development of the business in later years, the issues of the publishing house embraced an ampler and much more varied range. But William carefully treasured his father's private library. The spirit of the bibliomaniac developed itself in this special line, and the collection of old theological works included many choice specimens and rare editions of his father's favourite divines. They were latterly treasured in a cabinet at Hope Park, along with other relics on which William Nelson set a high value; and their loss on the destruction of the Hope Park Works in 1878 by fire was one of his greatest causes of regret. From his own choice collection of theological works, Mr. Thomas Nelson made his first selections; but after a time he realized the necessity of catering for the tastes of other

classes of readers; and so by-and-by there were added
to them " Robinson Crusoe," " Rasselas," " The Vicar of
Wakefield," Goldsmith's " Essays," his " Deserted Village," and other poems, along with popular favourites
of a like class.   Thus prosecuted, the business gradually expanded until the Bowhead establishment was no
longer sufficient for the accommodation required.

But free trade in books was in conflict with the
ideas inherited from the privileged guilds of elder
centuries.   Competition had hitherto been restricted
within narrow limits; and the daring innovator was
regarded by the regular trade with all the disfavour
of a revolutionist, against whom every effort was to be
employed to thwart the sale of his publications.   He
had accordingly to find other channels of trade.   Periodical visits were made to the smaller towns, over the
country, north and south, and beyond the Scottish border.   Thus a safe and extended business was gradually
established, destined ultimately to revolutionize the
book-trade.   By its means was inaugurated a system
of supply of popular literature, at prices within reach
of the masses, long before other publishers of this class
entered into competition on the same field.

The influences of early training are traceable throughout the whole of Mr. Thomas Nelson's career, and have
left their impress on the business which owed its origin
to his patient assiduity.   He remained to the last

faithful to the Covenanting Presbyterian Church, which maintained a stern adherence to the principles for which the martyrs of the Covenant had witnessed a good confession alike on the battlefield and the scaffold. His career in business had been an arduous struggle under many disabilities. As I remember him in my own boyhood, he was a grave, silent, yet not ungenial man; but one who seemed preoccupied with thoughts and cares in which a younger generation could claim no share. He had married, somewhat late in life, a bright young wife, by whom he had a family of four sons and three daughters; of whom the eldest son, the subject of this memoir, was born on the 13th of December, 1816.

On Mrs. Nelson the care and training of the young family devolved, as the successful prosecution of the business necessarily required the frequent and prolonged absence of their father. Yet his interest in them was not less fervent. An incident illustrative of this has also its bearings in relation to a characteristic feature of the devout faith of the old Covenanting fathers. He dreamt that a terrible accident had befallen his younger son John, then a youth of ten years of age, who was absent at Pettycur in Fife. He set off on the following morning, and crossed the Forth, burdened with foreboding visions of death. On his arrival, he learned that his boy had fallen into the sea, and been brought back apparently lifeless; but he had been revived, and then lay asleep after the exhaustion of this vital struggle. It fully accorded with the devout piety of the old Covenanter to recognize in his dream a divine message and proof of providential interposition.

Of Mrs. Nelson, Dr. John Cairns, who knew her intimately, refers, in his "In Memoriam" address on the death of this younger son, to her look of bright intelligence and winning affection, as indelibly impressed on the memory of all who were familiar with her. She possessed the happy mixture of tender, motherly guidance with an unusual amount of firmness and decision of character; and exercised great influence in the training of her son, who was passionately devoted to her. She was in perfect sympathy with her husband in his religious opinions, and venerated the memories of the confessors and martyrs of the Covenant; so that their sons and daughters were reared in strict conformity to the devout faith of Cameron, Peden, Cargill, and other fathers and confessors of that old Scottish type. Few men were more liberal-minded in later years than William Nelson; but the influence of early training survived through life, begetting some familiar traits of the best type of Scottish character evolved from that elder generation which so impressed the mind of the poet Wordsworth :—

" Pure livers were they all, austere and grave,
   And fcaring God ; the very children taught
   Stern self-respect, a reverence for God's Word,
   And a habitual piety, maintained
   With strictness scarcely kncwn on English ground."

Some characteristic manifestations of the results of such early training will come under review in the narrative of later years.

CHAPTER II

HAUNTS OF BOYHOOD.

THE curious ancient thoroughfare, the scene of early bookselling and publishing operations, has been described in the previous chapter: for many youthful recollections of William Nelson are associated with the West Bow. In those years Edinburgh was still the romantic town described by Scott in his " Marmion," piled steep and massy, close and high, along the ridge between the Cowgate and the Nor' Loch. Since then nearly all the antique historical mansions of the Castle Hill and the adjoining Bowhead have disappeared. An extensive range was swept away about 1835 in clearing the area for Johnston Terrace and the Assembly Hall of the Scottish Church. The famous old palace of Mary of Guise has given place to the rival Assembly Hall and the New College of the Free Church; and a broad highway now sweeps round the Castle rock where in early years antique lands, closes, and wynds, once the abodes of the

Scottish gentry, were crowded together on the slope reaching to the Grassmarket.

The fine timber-fronted tenement at the corner of the Bowhead, constructed mainly of oak, was a choice example of the burghers' dwellings in Old Edinburgh, with their trading booths opening on the street. Similar front lands in the High Street were the abodes of the merchants and traders. The " Gladstone Land " still stands near by in the Lawnmarket, bearing the initials of Thomas Gladstone, a merchant of Edinburgh in the days of Charles I. and Cromwell, to whose gifted descendant the restoration of the City Cross is due. The old nobles and landed gentry, judges and advocates, preferred the retirement of the closes and wynds, some of which still retain the names of patrician occupants. In one of those antique dwellings, in Trotter's Close, near the Bowhead, with its wainscotted chambers, painted panels, and other traces of older generations, the Nelson family resided in William's youth. The narrow approach to it admitted of no other carriage than the old-fashioned sedan chair; but the house itself was commodious, though with curious complexities of internal adaptation to its confined neighbourhood. One large chamber was shelved round, and stored with the surplus productions of publishing enterprise for which the Bowhead establishment had no room; and its miscellaneous contents furnished a

tempting resort for explorations into some strange fields
of literature not ordinarily lying within the range of
youthful studies. When at length the West Bow was
invaded by civic reformers, the Nelsons removed to a
more commodious house, the dwelling in an elder
century of Lady Elizabeth, Duchess of Gordon, while
the duke held the Castle for James II. The Gordon
House on the Castle Hill was a fine example of the
town mansions of the sixteenth century; and, owing to
its elevated site, commanded a beautiful view from its
southern windows, looking across the Grassmarket to
Heriot's Hospital, the Greyfriars' Churchyard, and the
distant range of the Pentland Hills. On its demolition, in 1887, William Nelson secured sundry interesting relics, including a landscape by James Norie,
which filled a panel over the mantlepiece in the
duchess's drawing-room. He also carried off the stone
gargoils, fashioned in the shape of cannons, which projected from under the south parapet; and they now
adorn the river wall of the garden at St. Bernard's
Well, the restoration of which, as will be seen hereafter, constituted one of the public-spirited works on
which he was engaged when his life drew to a close.

The stirring scene that the Grassmarket presented
on certain days, as a regular horse-fair, may be seen
in a fine engraving after Calcott in "The Provincial
Antiquities of Scotland;" and is still more graphi-

cally depicted in one of Geikie's humorous etchings. Here accordingly was a favourite resort of the boys from the neighbouring Bow. The Castle Esplanade at certain hours afforded a freer playground. At other times it offered the tempting attractions of military parade and drill. But Edinburgh has also within its civic bounds the royal park of Arthur's Seat, the Salisbury Crags, and Duddingston Loch, looking as though a choice fragment of the Highlands had been transported thither to form an adequate pleasure-ground for the Scottish capital. Hither flocked the city boys alike from the closes and wynds of the old town and from the new town crescents and squares. There was room for all, and a choice of sport for every age. Here is a reminiscence of a very youthful pastime, recalled in 1883, in a letter to Mr. James Campbell, one of William Nelson's old West Bow playmates:—"You will, I have no doubt, recollect a long, smooth stone near Jeanie Deans' House, in the Queen's Park. This stone was associated with my earliest recollections, as it was a great enjoyment for boys and girls to slide down it; and many a time, when I was a little boy, have I had this enjoyment. Well, the stone was in existence till only a few weeks ago, when some rascally fellows blew it to pieces with dynamite. The act is much to be regretted, as the stone, in addition to its being a source of enjoyment for little folks in the way

I have stated, was extremely interesting to geologists as one of the finest illustrations near Edinburgh of the polish produced by glacial action."

While the boys were disporting themselves on the Castle Hill and Arthur's Seat, without a care for the future, their father was grappling with the first difficulties inevitable to the innovator on the prescriptive usages of the book-trade. But whatever may have been the obstacles encountered by him, there was no grudging expenditure in the educational advantages provided for his sons. At the school of Mr. William Lennie, and subsequently at that of Mr. George Knight, then second to none in Edinburgh, and afterwards at the High School, William Nelson pursued his earlier studies; and there, too, some of the friendships were formed which he cherished with all the warmth of his sympathetic nature to the close of life. It was in those early days, at Mr. Knight's school, that the friendship was formed with his present biographer, along with George Wilson, subsequently Professor of Technology in the University of Edinburgh, with Dr. Philip Maclagan, and with William and James Sprunt, two young West Indians, the former of whom will reappear as British Consul in North Carolina. Of the more romantic career of the latter an account is happily preserved in the notes of an address by William Nelson at one of the gatherings of old schoolmates in later years, which

were so congenial to his tastes. After telling of James
Sprunt's first settlement in the island of St. Vincent
among a dissolute set of West Indians, his quitting it
for New Orleans, and being lost sight of for years, he
thus proceeds:—"He had landed penniless; but when
his old father and mother got their first letter from
him, it was an invitation for them to join him there
and share his good fortune. He next appears as rector
of a classical academy at Wilmington, North Carolina,
where he became a clergyman and pastor of the Presbyterian Church; and when the war broke out between
the North and South, he cast in his lot with the latter,
marched with the Wilmington brigade into action, and
as an army chaplain, under General Stonewall Jackson,
went through the terrible scenes of strife and carnage
in that bloody civil war, utterly regardless of danger,
and even ready to face death at the call of duty. His
popularity with his Wilmington congregation was not
lessened, it may be believed, when he returned to resume his pastoral charge at the close of the war." Of
other boys of those first school-days may be noted Dr.
J. A. Smith, in later years an active member of the
Royal Society, and Secretary of the Society of Antiquaries of Scotland; Dr. John Knight, the son of our
old teacher; the Rev. James Huie of Wooler, North-
umberland, and others, who formed themselves into
"The Juvenile Society for the Advancement of Know-

ledge," of which an account is given in the Memoir of
George Wilson by his sister.

The High School, a venerable civic institution dating
from the sixteenth century, still occupied the site of the
Blackfriars' Monastery, at the east end of the ridge
from which the ruined Kirk-of-Field was displaced by
the newly-founded university in Queen Mary's time.
The modern policeman had not yet superseded the old
city watch. The High School Wynd, a singularly
picturesque alley of timber-fronted lands, at the foot
of which stood the palace of Cardinal Beaton, gave
access to the Cowgate, a plebeian haunt, the young
roughs of which maintained a hereditary feud against
the "puppies" of the High School. A stray High
School boy, especially if he was a "guite" or fresh-
man, venturing into that Alsatia, incurred all the risks
of a wanderer into an enemy's lines; and from time to
time a bicker, or pitched battle with sticks and stones,
between the "puppies" of the High School and the
"blackguards" of the Cowgate, came off by mutual
understanding on a Saturday in the Hunter's Bog or
on the Links. The school numbered upwards of seven
hundred boys. The Yards, as the playground was
called, presented the busy scene characteristic of similar juvenile gatherings. But there was then less of re-
straint either by masters or police than under the new
régime of school boards and "peelers." Out of school

boys settled their own affairs, and righted their own wrongs, with results that seem to me on the whole to have tended to develop manliness and self-restraint. In the general sports, as well as in organized bickers or raids into the enemy's quarters, after some Cowgate encroachment upon the amenities of the school, all were one; but the acquaintance even with the boys of our own class was partial. They naturally formed into little groups of kindred spirits, the beginnings in some cases of life-long friendships.

Dr. Philip Maclagan, referring to those early school-days, says: "I was one of the original members of the Juvenile Society for the Advancement of Knowledge. The society met on Friday evening; papers were read by the members in rotation, and questions previously started were debated. I remember some of them—'Whether the whale or the herring afforded the more useful and profitable employment to mankind?' 'Whether the camel was more useful to the Arab or the reindeer to the Laplander?' and similar puzzles for youthful ingenuity." As yet political and social questions were unheeded; and the Saturday rambles, for which Edinburgh offers such rare advantages, furnished materials for subsequent discussion in diverse geological, botanical, and antiquarian subjects of interest. Those excursions extended to Cramond; to Royston Castle, picturesquely crowning a rock near the sea-shore; to Newhaven, Leith, or Portobello; or landward, to Craigmillar Castle, Corstorphine, Colinton, the Esk; and to the Braid or Blackford Hill: a stolen pleasure, since we were at that time liable to pursuit and ejection as trespassers. The Arthur's Seat as well as the Blackford Hill of those days, if less adapted for the proprieties of a city park, were more to the taste of youthful explorers while still in a state of nature. It was the Blackford of young Walter Scott—

> " On whose uncultured breast,
> Among the broom, and thorn, and whin,
> A truant boy, I sought the nest;
> Or listened, as I lay at rest,
> While rose on breezes thin
> The murmur of the city crowd."

Already, when Scott penned his "Marmion," the agriculturist and the builder were working havoc on the scene. How much more may survivors of that younger circle now say,—

> " O'er the landscape, as I look,
> Nought do I see unchanged remain,
> Save the rude cliffs and chiming brook.
> To me they make a heavy moan
> Of early friendships past and gone."

But such feelings found no place in the thoughts of the eager truants. Close at hand were the never-failing Calton Hill, or Arthur's Seat and Duddingston, with charm enough for a pleasant ramble, but also utilized, along with more extended excursions, for collecting specimens to furnish material for subsequent discussion in their Juvenile Society, as well as contributions to the museum which was already in course of formation.

The sea-shore had then, as in later years, a peculiar charm for William Nelson. To the very close of his life an excursion in company with some favourite companion to Newhaven, or to North Berwick, and off in one of the fishermen's boats to fish for haddock or whitings, furnished one of his most prized recreations. But it was at Kinghorn, his mother's birthplace, on the opposite shore of the Firth of Forth, that his choicest holidays were spent. In a letter written in long subsequent years to his old schoolmate and friend, the Rev. Dr. Simpson of Derby, when an event, hereafter referred to, brought him anew into intimate relations with the place, he thus recalls the memories of his early boyhood:—"My connection with Kinghorn has been very close; and my love for it, as my mother's birthplace, and the place where I spent many very happy days in my earliest years, and during my school holidays afterwards, is very great. I was exceedingly fond of fishing, both from the rocks on the sea-shore and at Kinghorn Loch; and happier days were never spent by any youngster than were those days of mine at Kinghorn. I knew every rock on the coast from Pettycur onwards to Seafield Tower on East the Braes, which is not far from the 'lang toon of Kirkcaldy;' and a finer sea-coast for grand rocks there is not anywhere on the northern coast of the Firth of Forth. I was as happy as I could be from morning till night. I remember the talks, too, in those early days by the old folks, which were principally about Paul Jones's visit to the Firth, my grandmother having seen his ship from the little hamlet of Glassmount, about two miles from Kinghorn, where she was born, and where her parents stayed at that time.

"Another favourite subject of talk was the 'windy Saturday,' a tremendous day of wind, when only one vessel, it was said, out in the Firth of Forth, was able to face the stormy blasts without coming to grief. A third subject of talk with the old folks was the mischief that steam-boats had done to the town, as, before they began to run, there were big boats to carry passengers; and as they started only at particular times of the tide, and did not go during the night, passengers had generally to stay some time in the town till the boats were ready to start—that is, for Leith, as there was no Newhaven in those days. 'What a good this did to the town!' and, 'What a mistake it was to upset the quiet, easy way of taking things, as they were in those good old days, by the introduction of

steam-boats!' My mother's uncle, John Macallum, was
the captain of the first steam-boat, or, at all events,
one of the first, that sailed on the Firth of Forth,
its name being the *Sir William Wallace.* It unfortunately was wrecked on some rocks near Burntisland.

"I could enlarge upon such themes to a great extent,
and upon my companions of those early days; but,
alas! those companions have all passed away, with two
exceptions—namely, Henry Darney, a worthy citizen
of Kinghorn, and Major Greig, now of Toronto, Canada.
My connection with Kinghorn came to a close about
1836, when my grandmother died; but such a liking
have I for the place, that I have paid it a short visit
almost every year since that time."

His more intimate relations with Kinghorn, as he
states, terminated with the death of his grandmother;
but his fondness for it remained through life. In 1885
his eldest sister, Mrs. George Brown, returned from
Canada, and I am indebted to her for some interesting
early reminiscences recalled by more than one visit
made in his company to their mother's birthplace. "It
was there," she writes, "he spent all his holidays as a
boy; and so eager was he to get to the place that the
very afternoon of the breaking up of school often saw
him on board the ferry-boat on his way across the
Forth, fishing-rod in hand and fishing-basket on back.

For fishing he had a perfect passion. At Newhaven, Kinghorn, Crail, North Berwick, and Oban, he was well known and greatly liked by all the fishermen, although frequently their patience must have been pretty well put to the test when they were taken out in rough weather by William, and they knew there were no fish to be had.

"When a boy at Kinghorn, late and early he might be seen either putting his tackle in order, or down on the beach digging for bait, or on the rocks, now on one and now on another, according to the state of the tide, contented to spend hours and hours together so that he only caught fish or even got what he called good nibbles. On many occasions he was so successful that he was able to keep the poor pretty well supplied with fish during his visits.

"It was not only during the holiday months that William occupied himself in fishing or in preparation for it. All through the winter he and his brothers spent a good deal of their time in manufacturing lines for the next summer's campaign. It is amusing to remember where materials for these fishing-lines sometimes came from. There was an old piano in the house which had seen better days, and the strings of it afforded a good supply of wire for fastening the hooks on the lines; the tail of any horse unfortunate enough to come in the way was put under contribution for a supply of hair. To the end of his life, his interest in and his love for Kinghorn never waned; and by the occasional visits he continued to pay, his acquaintance with the few remaining companions of his boyhood was kept up.

" The second last visit he paid was in 1886. My sister Jessie and I were with him. Leaving Edinburgh early in the day, we crossed to Burntisland; and getting a carriage there, we drove to Pettycur. His recollections were all of his boyhood. He showed us a part of the beach where he used to dig for cockles and sand-eels, and the rocks where he and his companions made a fire to roast potatoes. He pointed out the place where Alexander III. is said to have been killed; and re-called the old times of pinnaces and open boats before steamers were heard of. Leaving Pettycur, we drove to the loch, a lovely, sequestered place, where William caught his first pike. To show his love for fishing, my brother Tom recalls the fact that on one occasion, when the holidays were over and the day had come for William to return to Edinburgh, after he had fin-ished his preparations for starting, he looked at the clock, and saying he had still time to run up to the loch before the boat sailed, rushed off with his fishing-rod. Whether he came back with an empty basket or not tradition does not say. From the loch we made our way to the beautiful sandy beach; then up to the

Braes, where he used to scamper about, and on which there still stands an old hawthorn tree, by the side of which, he told us, he fired his first shot. He loved evidently to linger in memory over these days and recall his friends and playmates, the remembrance of whom brought tears to his eyes."

CHAPTER III.

SCHOOLS AND SCHOOLMATES.

WILLIAM NELSON was a pupil in the High School of Edinburgh when one great cycle in its history was completed. It had occupied the site of the old Blackfriars' Monastery for upwards of two hundred and seventy years. In 1555 the town house of Cardinal Beaton, at the foot of the Blackfriars' Wynd, which continued to be one of the most interesting historical buildings in Edinburgh till its demolition in 1871, was rented by the city for the use of the Grammar School, while a building for its permanent occupation was "being biggit on the east side of the Kirk-of-Field," the scene, a few years later, of Lord Darnley's mysterious assassination. Its rector was David Vocat, a prebendary of the neighbouring collegiate church of St. Mary-in-the-Field; and under his rule the cloisters of the Dominicans, built for them in 1230 by Alexander II., gave place to the halls and playground of the High School boys. But it was a turbulent age, and before the century closed the Yards became the scene of a tragic event which retained a prominent place among the traditions of the school so long as it remained on the old site. In 1598 Bailie Macmoran, one of the city magistrates, was shot in a barring out of the schoolboys by William Sinclair, a son of the Chancellor of Caithness. The contemporary diarist, Birrel, notes that "there was ane number of scholaris, being gentlemen's bairns, made a mutinie;" and on the poor bailie interposing, the schoolboy revolt ended in dire tragedy.

Great as were the changes that time had wrought on the locality where the old monastery of the Black Friars gave place to the City Grammar School, a flavour of historic antiquity pervaded it to the last. The episcopal palace of the Beatons, where the school work had been carried on for a time, still stood at the foot of the High School Wynd; and near by was the site of that of Gawain Douglas, who, while still provost of St. Giles's collegiate church—

> "In a barbarous age
> Gave to rude Scotland Virgil's page."

It was probably due to the vicinity of their lodgings that the poet interposed on behalf of the militant archbishop when, after the famous street feud of "Cleanse the Causeway," Beaton had vainly sought sanctuary behind the altar of the Blackfriars' Church, and, but

for the interposition of the poet, would have been slain.
His vigorous translation of the Æneid into the Scottish
vernacular was a favourite with William Nelson in
later years. But the associations of the locality in his
school days were for the most part of more recent
date.

The High School Yards had been the playground of
Hume, Robertson, Erskine, Horner, Jeffrey, Cockburn,
Brougham, and Scott, and of many a notability before
them. The memory of its gentle, scholarly rector,
Dr. Adam, author of " Roman Antiquities " and other
works, was still fresh; and the old school seemed
a link between past generations and the living age.
But neither the site, with its picturesque surroundings,
nor the building, accorded with the ideas of civic reformers who had organized a crusade against whatever
was out of keeping with the brand-new town. The
age had not then reverted to the mediæval models
which have since come into vogue. Classic art was
regarded as most suited to academic requirements; and
so a beautiful Grecian building—the finest specimen of
Thomas Hamilton's architectural skill, in the designing
of which his artist friend, David Roberts, was understood to have contributed valuable aid,—had been
erected on the southern slope of the Calton Hill, as a
more fitting home for the city Grammar School.

The migration from the antiquated building at the

head of the High School Wynd to this splendid edifice
in the New Town was an important change in many
ways besides the mere removal to more commodious
and sightly halls. It brought to an end a host of old
customs and traditions; and, among the rest, to the
hereditary feud between the Cowgate "blackguards"
and the High School "puppies." A grand civic ceremonial marked this transfer of the school to its
new domicile. On the 23rd of June 1829—a bright,
auspicious day—William Nelson, the head boy of
his class, with his schoolmates, under the leadership
of the rector and masters, walked in procession,
each bearing an osier wand, with music, military
escort, and all the civic glories that the Lord Provost
and magistrates could command, to do honour to the
occasion. It was a memorable epoch in schoolboy
life. But it seemed to the old boys as though they
never were quite at home in their stately New Town
quarters. Old "Blackie," with her famous "gib" or toffy
stall, was out of place there; and as for Brown's famous
subterranean pie-shop in the old High School Wynd, it
necessarily tarried behind, to the inevitable ruin of a
once flourishing business. Not the building only, but
the entire scholastic system carried on within its walls,
soon after underwent a complete revolution; and the
work of the venerable Grammar School of Prebendary
Vocat, the classic arena of Adam, Pillans, and Carson,

has since devolved on Fettes College, a creation of the present century.

But the old classic system still prevailed in William Nelson's time; and, notwithstanding some glaring defects, was turned by him to good account. As to the school itself, it must be owned that it stood in need of reform. The class of Mr. Benjamin Mackay, under whose training William Nelson remained for four years, numbered upwards of a hundred boys. Those in the two front forms worked with more or less persistency under a somewhat coercive system; the remainder idled in the most flagrant fashion, and not a few of them looked back in later years on those dreary hours with an indignant sense of wasted time. But William Nelson was foremost among the studious workers. The same quiet, resolute perseverance which marked his later career in business characterized him as a schoolboy. He maintained his place as the dux of his class, carried off the chief prizes of the school, and at the close of his course under the rector, Dr. Carson, he passed to the university with the highest honours, as classical gold medalist.

Among the carefully preserved papers of his early years are a bundle of old letters from schoolmates, enclosed in an envelope addressed to his mother, with an endorsation begging her to see to their safe keeping. They furnish pleasant glimpses of the affectionate rela-

tions already established with more than one of the
friends of later years.   The solemn protest of the
learned Principal, Dr. Lee, against "that most ob-
jectionable and pernicious practice of making balls of
snow," is humorously commented on, along with graver
matters, such as pertained to the themes and discussions
of the Juvenile Literary Society, and the more ambitious debating societies of the university.   His own
sense of humour found free play both in early and later
years; but above all, his youthful letters are full of
pleasant gossip of the old sailors of Kinghorn, who told
him yarns of the victories in which they had shared
in the great French war, and the pranks they indulged
in when flush with prize-money.   Old Charlie Mackenzie had been in the *Mars* in her action with the
Hercules, one of the bloodiest naval conflicts of the
war.   Another of the Kinghorn story-tellers—Orrock,
who died in 1836, upwards of ninety years of age—
claimed to have known the man who acted as drummer
at the Porteous mob, and to have learned from him
some details of the burning of the doors, and so gaining
admission to the Tolbooth.   The intense feeling of local
attachment which such reminiscences reveal manifested
itself in later years in the interest he took in improvements at Kinghorn, as well as in the more costly restorations in his native city.   But one of the first fruits of
his intercourse with the old pensioners of Kinghorn,

who, as he says, "were great fishers for podlies from
certain rocks on the sea-shore," was the capture of a
crab with a double claw, a *lusus naturæ*, which furnished a novel subject for discussion at a meeting of
the Juvenile Literary Society. His contributions to its
collections and learned discussions were generally of
the same class—algæ, shells, or other marine curiosities,
the fruits of his last holiday ramble by the sea.

Among stray waifs that have survived from those
old days is a letter, bearing date February 20, 1829,
addressed to the secretary of the Juvenile Society by
the elder brother of one of its members. With all the
condescension of an undergraduate placing his mature
knowledge at the service of schoolboys, the writer sets
forth " the very great pleasure I take in hearing of
the proceedings of your society, and my unqualified
approbation of your plan of keeping a journal as a sort
of record of your proceedings." He proceeds: "I daresay you are unaware that the duties of a student of
medicine are of a very arduous nature." But, as he
goes on to state, he had laid before the Plinian Society
in the previous summer a paper on certain " Discoveries
made behind Edinburgh Castle in digging the foundation of the new bridge,"—part of the terraced road
which involved the destruction of Trotter's Close and
the Nelson homestead,—and this, he says, "I shall copy
out in a style which I hope will prove interesting to

my young friends, and which may, perhaps, form a contribution to their journal." The writer, whose seniority, by the years that separate the College student from the High School boy, entitled him thus condescendingly to address his brother Philip and the other juvenile *savants*, is now Sir Douglas Maclagan, the genial veteran Professor of Medical Jurisprudence in his own university; and, it may be added, the author of some of the most popular of a younger generation's student-songs.

At a later stage the juvenile debaters awoke to an interest in the stirring questions of the day. Mr. Alexander Sprunt, writing from Wilmington, North Carolina, in 1859, says: "During the period of our High School curriculum, questions were occupying the public mind, and startling events taking place in Europe: the final struggle of the Poles, the French 'Three Days of July,' the reform movement, etc. The subject of the immediate or gradual emancipation of the negro slaves in the colonies was also keenly discussed about that time. Some of us, being related to families of the colonists, were familiar with the arguments for a gradual abolition of slavery." William Nelson took up the question warmly, and was an uncompromising advocate for immediate emancipation. As to the oft-renewed struggle in France between Bourbon Royalists, Imperialists, and Red Republicans, it was forcibly brought home to the realization of the young debaters by the presence of the exiled Charles X. and his little court at Holyrood; and by the occasional sight of the royal refugee as he passed the High School Yards on foot, in company with one or two of his suite, to enjoy the magnificent panorama from the Calton Hill.

The fruits of those early experiences could be discerned in later years. The boy's education was progressing under other teachings besides those of the schoolmaster. It was altogether alien to the unobtrusiveness of William Nelson's sensitive nature to take, in later years, a prominent share in political life; but his generous support was extended in the most practical form to all philanthropic movements. He manifested the keenest interest in all questions of liberal politics: in the emancipation of the slaves; in the prolonged controversies which led to the disruption of the Scottish Church; and in the more recent struggle between the Slave and Free States in the great American Civil War. Most of those questions belong to periods long subsequent to the time when James and Alexander Sprunt were the champions of the West Indian planters, and William Nelson and other juvenile debaters maintained the cause of the enslaved negro.

But the members of the Literary Society, as already noted, had their field-days as well as their Friday night sessions; and in pursuit of material for their papers, as well as in the free use of the Saturday and other holidays, the schoolmates had many an exciting ramble. In spite of its uncertain climate, Edinburgh presents an unequalled variety of choice holiday excursions; and as to the rain, it required a good deal more than an ordinary shower to put a stop to any projected excursion. In walking, climbing, and all the ordinary feats of healthy boyhood, William Nelson was unsurpassed. To make our way to the summit of Salisbury Crags by the famous Cat-Nick, or outrival each other in the attempt to scale Samson's Ribs, and sit supreme on some overhanging ledge of the basaltic columns, were among the most favourite pastimes. Or a leisurely climb along the slopes to the summit of Arthur's Seat, and a survey of the magnificent landscape spread out to view, were a prelude, at the word, to a dash down the hill, scrambling like so many goats over the western cliffs and the rough slope below, and so by the Hunter's Bog, for the first draught at St. Anthony's Well. In all such feats William Nelson was a match for any schoolmate. His coolness equalled his courage, and he had a love for daring feats such as those who only knew him in later years will hardly realize. When the old home at the Bowhead was displaced by the Assembly Hall, and its lofty spire was in process of erection, he made friends with the contractor, and I accompanied him in more than one ascent. A steam hoist carried us up the main portion of the way; and then came the trying ordeal on the ladders. But as the tapering spire approached completion, it was no longer possible to reach the summit from within; and I still recall with vividness the composure with which, all unconscious of danger, he walked out on the narrow plank, over a depth of upwards of two hundred feet, and stood at the extreme end of it, noting and commenting on the various objects spread out below.

A future career for life was as yet unthought of. But while aiming solely at pleasure, and rejoicing in a holiday's escape from school, the boy was unconsciously educating himself. Already the botanical box and the geological hammer were in vogue. Not, indeed, the luxurious appliances with which amateur naturalists are now furnished. Any hammer sufficed for getting at a coveted fossil; and as for our *hortus siccus*, an old candle-box was appropriated by the botanical collector. But the archæological tastes in which more than one of William Nelson's schoolmates sympathized, and to which he gave such practical expression in later years, were already in process of development. The pleasurable associations with historic scenes and picturesque ruins found ample scope in those holiday rambles. Craigmillar Castle was close at hand; and within easy distance was old Roman Cramond, with chances of a numismatic prize to the fortunate explorer, and with the sculptured eagle of the legionaries of the second century still visible on the cliff at the mouth of the river Almond. This had a special charm for boys fresh from their Cæsar and Tacitus, giving a sense of reality to those forgotten centuries. It was an object-lesson, better even than the Roman altar dedicated to the goddess Epona—DEÆ EPONÆ—which Dr. Carson, the Rector of the High School, produced to his class, and won their attentive admiration as he pointed to the focus in which the Roman horse-jockey had poured a libation; and adduced passages from the Satires of Juvenal in confirmation of his theme.

Farther afield lay Woodhouselee, Seton and Roslin chapels; Niddry, Borthwick, and Crichton castles; Preston Cross and Tower; and many another storied ruin associated with familiar historic events. Pinkie Cleugh, Carberry Hill, Lasswade, Dalkeith, and Prestonpans, were each linked with song or story. Maclagan was an ardent collector of plants and insects; geology divided with botany the interest of George Wilson; John A. Smith had already begun the collection of coins; and William Nelson was forming the tastes which manifested themselves in later years in his love for every venerable nook of his native city, and in his zeal for the preservation of its historic memorials.

The change from school to college life is in every case an important one. With the majority it involves emancipation, in a large degree, from enforced and distasteful studies, and their exchange for congenial pursuits. The youth begins for the first time to estimate knowledge at its real worth, and to shape out plans of study for himself. But the novel arena is no less important as that in which the companionships of the playground give place to that discriminating choice of congenial associates in which life-long friendships have so often originated. It is the joyous season in which the springtide is just merging into life's early summer; when youth is animated by all generous aspirations, and hope's rainbow arch spans the horizon.

The period of William Nelson's admission as an undergraduate of the University of Edinburgh was in some respects a brilliant one in its history; and even more so in relation to its students than its professors. Dr. John Lee, the learned Church historian and black-letter scholar, was principal, and Dr. Chalmers occupied the chair of divinity; the chair of natural philosophy was successively occupied by Sir John Leslie and by James D. Forbes. Before the abrupt close of William Nelson's academic career, Sir William Hamilton had assumed the lead in its school of mental science; and the fame of John Wilson, its professor of moral philosophy, under his pseudonym of "Christopher North," attracted many to his class-room for whom his professed theme would have had no charm.

But in the department of classics, for which all William Nelson's previous training had been specially directed, the faculty was imperfectly equipped. Dunbar, a poor representative of Hellenic scholarship, had then filled the Greek chair for upwards of a quarter of a century. On the other hand, the professor of humanity was James Pillans, an elegant scholar, and, in the words of Sir Alexander Grant, "a born teacher and educator;" though latterly more prone to dwell on little critical niceties than to give himself up to the drudgery which was indispensable for the training of his large and often inadequately prepared class. Among other traits that his old pupils will recall was the never-failing protest at the opening of a new session, which reminded the class that he enjoyed the dubious fame of being pilloried by Byron in his "English Bards and Scotch Reviewers." The irate bard, in his indiscriminate *furor*, had characterized the professor of humanity as "Paltry Pillans;" and William Nelson used to quote this incident of his own experience in justification of the title:—He had an essay to give in on a certain day, and not having finished it till late on the previous night, instead of walking to the professor's remote residence at Inverleith Row, he dropped his manuscript into the nearest post-box. Next day, when the class assembled, the first intimation from the professor was, "I will thank Mr. William Nelson to hand twopence to

the janitor for the postage of his essay!" Notwithstanding some amusing eccentricities, Professor Pillans
was held in great esteem by his old pupil as an apt and
painstaking enthusiast in his profession; and the good
feeling was mutual. William Nelson was a favourite
pupil, in whose progress he took a lively interest, and
it was in spite of his most urgent remonstrances that
the classic muse was abandoned at the call of filial
duty.

But it was the fortune of William Nelson, in those
happy days of student life, to find himself among a
rare band of undergraduates, many of whom subsequently won a name for themselves in ampler fields.
Edward Forbes was then a zealous volunteer on the
staff of the *University Maga*, contributing with pen
and pencil, in prose and verse, to its columns. He had
a rare power of winning co-operation in whatever he
set on foot; and he gathered around him a band of
kindred spirits, who, as sharers in the exuberant frolic
and satire of the *Maga*, formed themselves at length
into the Magi, or members of the Maga Club. Out of
this grew the famous "Brotherhood of the Friends of
Truth," with its archimagus, its ribbon, and its mystic
motto :—

ΟΙΝΟΣ ΕΡΩΣ ΜΑΘΗΣΙΣ,

which still survives under its later guise of the Red

Lions of the British Association gatherings. There was a curious admixture of youthful exuberance and frolic with a lofty earnestness of aim in the Brotherhood. The search after truth was declared, in its programme, not only to be man's noblest occupation, but his duty; and the spirit of the order is thus set forth: "This brotherhood is a union of the searchers after truth, for the glory of God, the good of all, and the honour of the order, to the end that mind may hold its rightful sway in the world."

Of the youthful band of undergraduates, John Goodsir, Bennett, Blackie, Lyon Playfair, George Wilson, and Edward Forbes, all ultimately filled chairs in their own university. Day succeeded to a professorship in St. Andrews, and Struthers to one in Aberdeen. Henry Goodsir, a youth of high ability, accompanied Sir John Franklin as naturalist in the ill-fated Arctic expedition, from which none returned. Dr. Stanger distinguished himself, with better fortune, in the Niger expedition of 1844; Andrew Ramsay rose to be chief of the Geological Survey; and other fellow-students and members of the order have occupied professors' chairs in Canada and in India, have represented their university in Parliament, or made their mark in no less useful ways. Among the latter the name of William Nelson claims an honourable rank. For the scheme of the brotherhood required each member "to devote his time and his energies to the department for which he feels and proves himself best fitted, communicating his knowledge to all, so that all may benefit thereby, casting away selfishness, and enforcing precepts of love." Assuredly when those maxims came to be tested in the daily business of life, no one gave their spirit of unselfishness more practical manifestation than the subject of this memoir.

In Professor Pillans's class he maintained the standing which he had achieved at the High School. His foremost but unequal rival in the composition of Latin verse was the late George Paxton Young, the esteemed Professor of Logic and Metaphysics in the University of Toronto. It was while William Nelson was still a student that John Cairns—the friend and fellow-student both at Edinburgh and Berlin of his younger brother, John Nelson, and now the venerable Principal and Professor of Systematic Theology in the Divinity Hall of the United Presbyterian Church—came fresh from the pastoral hills of Berwickshire to win for himself a distinguished place among the men of his time.

Amid the stimulus and rivalry of such competitors for fame, the young student devoted himself with renewed zeal to the classics, with undefined visions of some honourable professional or academic reward as his life-prize; and fulfilled the high anticipations of his earlier career. But while thus steadily pursuing a

course which gave abundant promise of triumph, his
father was suddenly prostrated by disease; and William,
as the eldest son of a large family, abandoned all the
bright prospects of his university career, and the dream
of professional or academic achievements, to grapple
with the unfamiliar difficulties of a commercial enterprise, till then conducted on a scale commensurate with
the modest aims of an elder generation in the Old
Town of Edinburgh.

The business of Mr. Thomas Nelson was a curious
survival of the system borrowed from the great fairs
of the Middle Ages, and grafted on to their older traffic
by the successors of Guttenburg and Fust; of Caxton,
Wynkin de Worde, and Chepman and Miller. Allan
Ramsay had followed in their steps, with his booth at
the sign of the Mercury, opposite the head of Niddry's
Wynd, from whence he transferred it to the Lucken-
booths at the City Cross. It was in just such another
luckenbooth at the Bowhead that Mr. Thomas Nelson
originated the business which has since developed into
such great proportions.

William Nelson threw himself at once, with characteristic singleness of aim, into his new vocation; nor
did he ever express regret at his enforced desertion
of scholarship for trade. But few men have carried
away from school or college a keener sense of the
attachments of student life. To the last the plea of

an old schoolmate ever presented an irresistible claim
which scarcely any demerit could cancel. The fate of
one whose life, by his own misconduct, had closed in
miserable failure is thus charitably noted in one of his
letters: "Poor —— died two days ago of congestion of
the lungs; and it is a wonder that he hung on so long,
as he has been in a very dilapidated condition for years.
The last time I saw him, his condition was truly pitiable. I sent him a fresh bolster and bedding, for the
ones he had were hard and foul. Poor fellow! he did
a great deal to hasten the approach of the last enemy."
His loyalty to early friends was unfailing. He kept a
record of his classmates in the High School, and noted
with keenest interest their success or failure in life.
He told with kindly humour of the refusal of a liberal
"tip" offered to a porter at Cairo who had been specially
serviceable, and then claimed fellowship by reminding
him of old High School doings. B—— was the ne'er-
do-weel of Mackay's class, who had thus found his
vocation in the land of the Pharaohs. His sympathy
was unbounded in any honour or good fortune achieved
by a schoolmate; and latterly, as he watched the rapidly
diminishing numbers of the old group of school and college companions, he recorded at the close of each year
the minutes of Death's roll-call. To one who entered
so keenly into academic life, and whose career was so
replete with promise, it was a trying ordeal to abandon

college for the uncongenial drudgery of a trading venture for which such experiences seemed to promise no helpful training. But in Scotland a university career is by no means regarded as unsuitable preparation for trade and commerce; and William Nelson was speedily to show what success the classical gold medalist of the High School and the best writer of Latin verse in the College could achieve in business life.

CHAPTER IV.

THE CASTLE HILL.

WITH characteristic energy the young student, now in his nineteenth year, set himself to grapple with the novel difficulties of the book-trade. Neither the irksome drudgery nor the uncongenial demands incident to the business daunted the youthful adventurer, who had so recently found his highest vocation in the mastery of Latin quantities, and the triumphs of competitive hexameters after the models of Horace and Virgil. In the summer of 1880, the present writer spent some weeks with his old schoolmate at Philiphaugh, in the vale of Yarrow, famous as the scene of Montrose's last battle. During an excursion to Berwick, with the special object of visiting another schoolmate, he pointed out more than one book-store in the old Border town, familiar to him in association with his first experiences as a commercial traveller, and humorously described those early ventures in the disposal of his literary wares. According to Johnson of Liverpool, his journey extended to that city, and Mr.

Johnson gave him his first large order for books. He had already succeeded in overcoming the prejudices of the regular trade, and fixed a scale of prices which disarmed their antagonism.

The books, as already stated, were for the most part reprints from standard and popular works beyond the range of copyright restrictions. Their paper-covered boards and imperfect printing were in striking contrast to the choice typography, paper, and binding, and the tasteful illustrations, which characterized the works issued by the firm in later days. Yet the germ even of this was already discernible in the engraved frontispieces and vignette titles introduced to catch the eye and cater for the popular taste.

So early as 1829, Mr. Thomas Nelson, senior, had aimed at the extension of his business by engaging a commercial traveller to push the sales of his publications with the trade. Mr. James Macdonald was first despatched on this mission; but as Curwen states, in his "History of Booksellers," owing to the stigma attached to the unwonted nature of the business, his mission was a failure. "At Aberdeen the booksellers rose up in arms, and only one had the courage to give him an order." To him succeeded, ere long, Mr. James Peters, a more successful agent, and a faithful *attaché* of the house through all its later fortunes till his death. But Curwen says: "It was not until Mr. William Nelson, the eldest son of the founder, took to the road that the trade business was really consolidated, not only in Scotland, but also in the chief towns of the United Kingdom. In fact, it may be said that Mr. William Nelson was the real builder of the business, working upwards from a foundation that was certainly narrow and circumscribed. Mr. Thomas Nelson, the younger brother, soon after this admitted to the firm, undertook the energetic superintendence of the manufacturing department, and was the originator of the extensive series of school books."

William Nelson's taste in literature was refined, and his reading extensive. His mind was stored with the fruits of years of liberal study; and when stimulated by the sight of beautiful scenery, or moved by some unusual occurrence, he sometimes surprised strangers by his apt and lengthened quotations from favourite poets. Soon after the removal to the Castle Hill establishment, Mr. Duncan Keith,—the son of an old friend of Mr. Nelson, with whom William had spent at Glasgow a brief period of initiation into the mysteries of trading,—was welcomed as a member of the West Bow home-circle, and took his place among the busy corps on the Castle Hill. He was the junior of William Nelson by some years, and thus writes: "My evenings were chiefly spent in the society of the younger branches of the family; but I have a distinct remembrance of William reading aloud from Horace and Virgil in a manner that showed an intimate acquaintance with the language, and an appreciation of the poetry in the original. Though a High School dux myself, it was far above me ; and, so far as my later observation goes, above most people." But it was only amongst intimate friends that he gave free play to his literary sympathies. Nothing was more remote from his character than any effort at display ; and men of culture who, in their intercourse with him, had long regarded him only as the man of business, were sometimes startled by an unexpected betrayal of his familiarity with classical and general literature, as well as by his sound judgment on questions of critical discussion.

With a taste thus matured, his feeling for art was refined, and he directed his efforts, with ingenious skill, to render the works issued from the firm attractive. Novel methods of illustration were introduced. Woodcuts were printed with tinted grounds and relieved lights. Chromo-lithographs vied in effect with the original water-colour drawings. A late series of reproductions of Landseer's pictures, though designed only for a child's book, constituted a valuable memorial of the great animal painter. Inventive ingenuity was directed to the production of fresh novelties in binding and illustration, many of which were eagerly copied by the trade. William Nelson's appreciation of artistic excellence seemed to be innate and instinctive. "A thing of beauty" was a joy to him wholly apart from his own share in its production. His admiration for a well-got-up book, or for illustrations of unusual excellence, found as hearty utterance in reference to the publications of another firm as of his own; and hence he was always open to fresh hints, and prepared for improvement on his most successful efforts. He was, indeed, too easily beguiled by good looks both in books and men. This characteristic passage occurs in a letter to an old friend: "I had a call two days ago from a most fair-spoken English clergyman, who wanted help to build a ragged school in Sheffield. He insisted that you had introduced him to me, and that I had taken him over the works and given him a book, which was likely enough; though, as I told him, I had no recollection of it. He was most plausible, and very good-looking. A good-looking outside takes my fancy in anything. I always find myself expecting the best of a good-looking book; and I am apt to believe pleasant things of good-looking people also. He assured me he was a great friend of yours; and he had such a friendly look that I gave him what he wanted. Do you know anything of this Dr. Pike? I have had my suspicions of him that he is a plausible humbug,"—which, as in many a similar case, proved to be only too well founded.

5

A writer in the *Scottish Typographical Circular*
remarks: " Mr. Nelson was often popping in and out
among artists and engravers who did work for him,
giving them new ideas and further suggestions. He
did not grudge trouble or expense if he got things nice
and to his mind. He rejoiced in beautiful typography,
and displayed great artistic taste in the wood-cuts and
illustrations." He was indeed a familiar visitor in the
studios of London and Paris, as well as of Edinburgh ;
and during his frequent Continental tours derived intense pleasure from his visits to the galleries both of
ancient and modern art. His eye was quick to discern
the merits of a painting, and his judgment was prompt
and decided. He was indeed sensitive to any manifestation of bad taste ; and the unsightly disfigurement
of the buildings or thoroughfares of his native city by
placards or signboards, excited his anger to a degree
that sometimes startled the offender. His remonstrance
on such occasions was apt to be expressed with a blunt
sincerity that could not be misunderstood. The same
severe standard of taste was applied in his own business, and made its influence felt in every department
of typography, illustration, and binding.

A memorandum, found among his papers after his
death, preserves an incident in the first stages of the
inexperienced but energetic reformer's proceedings.
His father had acquired a set of stereotype plates of

Drinkwater's "Siege of Gibraltar," and had a portrait of its author engraved for the frontispiece. A reprint of it being in progress, the plate was intrusted to the engraver for retouching ; and he undertook to get the autograph of the old soldier, to be added as an attractive feature. The new and illustrated edition was issued accordingly, and found a ready sale. But some years afterwards a venerable military-looking gentleman waited on Mr. Nelson, and asked where he had obtained the signature. Colonel Drinkwater, who was supposed to have been long since dead, was himself the questioner ; and, as William Nelson notes, the signature was subsequently identified as in the handwriting of the deceased manager of Mr. Lizar's engraving establishment. But only in the first stage of transition from student life to the counting-house and the publisher's office could such a proceeding have eluded his vigilance. A copy of the engraving is attached to the memorandum, and contrasts very markedly with the illustrations of later years, when William Nelson's critical taste, conjoined with his experience in adapting the issues of his publishing-house to popular demand, won for the productions of the firm a character for great attractiveness in outward aspect and illustration. At a later date, the "Chronicles of the Schönberg-Cotta Family" constituted the first of a highly popular series of books by the same author.

The charming authoress who writes under the initials
A. L. O. E., the late Mary Howitt, Mrs. Traill, R. M.
Ballantyne, and other writers, figured on their list of
authors. The charming series of "Art Gift Books,"
from the French of M. Jules and Mme. Michelet, and
M. Arthur Mangin—"The Insect," "The Bird," "The
Mysteries of the Ocean," and "The Desert World," as
well as other works of the same class—are illustrated
in the best style of art. But it was as caterers for
the people, in an abundant supply of pure, high-toned
popular literature, and not as rivals of the great publishing houses through which the most eminent writers
appeal to select classes of readers, that the Nelsons
achieved their greatest success. In the tribute paid to
the worth of William Nelson by the Rev. Dr. Alison
when his life-work was finished, it is said: "His influence, and that of the firm of which he was the head,
has gone forth healthfully to the ends of the earth.
Religious principle, no less than skill and taste and
enterprise, has been in all their work as publishers of
literature. No man can measure the good which that
incessant stream of excellent books issuing from their
press has done for the world. To a large extent they
have been for the multitude, rather than for the learned
few." But this was the summing up of the work of a
lifetime. Much had to be achieved in its progress, step
by step, ere such results could even be aimed at.

Under the energetic management of the young publisher the picturesque tenement at the head of the West Bow, which had sufficed for his father's bookselling operations, soon proved inadequate for the growing business. A neighbouring "land,"—as an entire pile of building in the Old Town of Edinburgh is still called, —situated at the head of Blyth's Close, Castle Hill, with the palace of Mary of Guise in its rear, was secured; and there the first steps were taken which ultimately developed into the great establishments of Hope Park and Parkside. Machinery was brought into use wherever available; and a well-organized division of labour was introduced, until at length nearly every process, from the initial type-setting to the final issue of the bound and illustrated volume, was executed on the premises. The locality where this new departure was made, preparatory to the great works at Hope Park, with its hundreds of work-people, and its wholesale branches at London and New York, is one rich in literary associations. Near by, on the northern slope of the Castle bank, is the house of Allan Ramsay, poet and bookseller; Blair's Close, long noted among the most ancient nooks of the Castle Hill, was the abode of Alison Cockburn, authoress of "The Flowers of the Forest," and of other plaintive as well as humorous Scottish songs. To St. James's Court, on the east side, James Boswell brought Dr. Samuel Johnson, and entertained him in the house where he had succeeded to the historian David Hume. There was an old-world literary flavour about the place that gave a certain piquancy to the start of the young adventurer deserting the classic grove for the prosaic haunts of commerce.

The Rev. Dr. Simpson of Derby, already noted as an old schoolmate and a life-long friend, refers in one of his letters to the lectures and social entertainments provided at a later date for the numerous workers in the Hope Park establishment, in which he was an active labourer. But the interest taken by William Nelson in his employés was manifested at an earlier stage. Lectures and social recreations had already been instituted before the transfer of the works to Hope Park, in some of the earliest of which the present writer bore a part. But with increasing numbers, and more ample room, those instructive entertainments were organized on an extensive scale, and are described in a memorandum of Dr. Simpson, by whom many of the later lectures were given. His account of them may find a fit place here, though in some points it anticipates the narrative of later years. "The deep interest," he remarks, "which Mr. Nelson felt in his work-people, and his desire to promote their well-being in every sense, conspicuously appear in the entertainments which were from time to time got up for them. At first these were chiefly in the nature of banquets or suppers, to which all were invited, when they were regaled with the good things of this life in a judicious but liberal manner. Along with this, however, he was careful to combine moral and religious instruction, by securing addresses by one or two clerical friends. By-and-by he provided for them occasional lectures on subjects of varied interest. For those he got up, at considerable expense and trouble, a series of illustrations which were shown on a screen by the oxy-hydrogen light, the lecturer describing each picture while it was before the eyes of the audience. This was, I believe, the first introduction of this form of lecture, which has since become so common. The pictures were reproduced from engravings by the photographer of the establishment, Mr. Sinclair, and then hand-coloured with much care and skill by Mr. Ramage, who devoted himself to the art-work connected with the extensive business of the firm.

"The first of those illustrated lectures was on the transfer of Napoleon's remains from St. Helena to Paris. The second was on Garibaldi's invasion of Sicily and Italy, ending with his meeting with Victor Immanuel, and hailing him as king of Italy. Afterwards a new departure was made, and the lectures were chiefly devoted to the genius and works of celebrated artists; the illustrations being transcripts of the artists' principal works. The first subject of this class was David Scott, R.S.A., in connection with his illustrations of Coleridge's 'Ancient Mariner,' subsequently reproduced by Messrs. Nelson in a tasteful edition of the poem. The next lecture was devoted to the works of Landseer; and to this succeeded similar illustrations of Hogarth, Wilkie, Harvey, Leech, etc. Those lectures were greatly appreciated; the large hall at Hope Park, in which they were given, being always crowded to excess by the employés, their wives and families, supplemented by friends invited by Mr. Nelson, including some who took an active part in this generous effort for the social elevation of the working-classes, such as Dr. Guthrie and Dr. Hannah; and their artist friends, Sir George Harvey, D. O. Hill, James Drummond, and others. For each of those lectures Mr. Nelson had prepared from twenty to thirty slides, which were arranged in partitioned cases made for their safe keeping." But they perished, along with much more valuable property, in the disastrous fire of 1878.

But only the initial steps towards the full development of the Hope Park works, with their ingeniously devised machinery and systematic division of labour, were possible at the Castle Hill establishment. Its accommodation, though a great step in advance of that at the Bowhead, was inadequate for such plans, and the numbers employed were correspondingly limited. But the workmen were carefully selected; and from the first the relations between them and their employer were characterized by mutual respect and confidence. They recognized in him one whose interest in their welfare was generous, and his sympathy that of a friend. But his own attention to business extended to the minutest details, and anything indicative of mere eye-service or sloth was intolerable to him. An anecdote highly characteristic of him is thus narrated on the authority of one who had been long in his employment:—"Two navvies were engaged one day at Hope Park turning a crank when Mr. William Nelson was passing. He paused for a moment and looked at the men, who seemed to go about their work rather leisurely. He then came forward to them, and asked, in a gruff manner, if they could not work a little harder and turn the crank quicker. They answered at once 'they could not; it was a stiff job, and very fatiguing.' 'Nonsense,' he replied; 'let me try.' Seizing one of the handles, he did try; but, after giving the handle two or three turns, desisted, for it made the perspiration pour from him. Then he remarked, 'Ay, just go on as you've been doing;' and, putting his hand into his pocket, added, 'There's half-a-crown between you.' Many similar anecdotes might be told. He liked smart, active workmen; but he did not willingly drive or unduly

press any one. He would at once rebuke any of his
employés if he considered they deserved it; but if
afterwards he found he had acted hastily or wrongly,
he would apologize, even to the humblest worker, and
almost invariably with the apology there came a gift."

It is not surprising that the relations between such
an employer and his workmen were something closer
than those of the mere hireling. The workmen who
had shared in his first efforts in the Castle Hill establishment followed him to Hope Park. Some of them,
by their fidelity and skill, contributed to the success of
later years; and the veteran survivors of that original
staff were regarded by William Nelson to the last as
objects of exceptional favour.

Among those who thus migrated from the Castle
Hill to Hope Park, one claims special attention as a
relic of the original Bowhead establishment. James
Peters has already been named. He was a man of
good education, and, what was rare in his day, had a
familiar knowledge of the French language. He was,
moreover, a devout Presbyterian of the early type,
eschewing the Covenanting exclusiveness of his old
master, and holding faithfully to the National Kirk.
His familiarity with the Scriptures was so great that
he was accredited with knowing the entire New Testament by heart, and quoting familiarly from much of
the Old Testament. He had been the trusted clerk,

commercial traveller, and man of all work: the entire staff for a time of the bookselling business under the elder *régime;* and as the cautious ventures of its founder gave way to the comprehensive schemes of a younger generation, he watched their operations with many misgivings. Old Peters would have furnished a study for Sir Walter Scott fit to have ranked alongside of his Owen and Caleb Balderstone. He moved in all things with the regularity of clockwork, and sternly resented in others the slightest deviation from orderly business procedure or punctuality as to time. Mr. Duncan Keith sums up his own early recollections of him with the remark that "even John Munro, the beadle of Mr. Goold the Covenanting minister's kirk, stood in awe of him." One day, contrary to all precedent, he asked leave to go away a little earlier than the usual closing hour. He reappeared next morning, and, addressing William, said, "I wish you would tell your father I got married yesterday." On inquiry, he stated that he had just wedded the elderly dame with whom he lodged. "It will be cheaper," he said; "and we'll get on weel enough thegither. We hae been lang used to each other." When in early days the plan of book sales was in vogue, he was intrusted with the carrying out of one of the ventures; but his ideas of orderly procedure were wholly at variance with the novel experiment. He abruptly returned home the following day, and would have nothing more to do with such work. His loyalty to his young masters knew no bounds; but he could never quite forget that they had been boys when he had the sole charge of the Bowhead buith, or indeed feel it to be natural to speak of them otherwise than by their Christian names. Duty clearly required him to advise and warn them at every new step, so unlike the prudent thrift of early days. If we could realize all the feelings of a sober old brood-hen when the ducklings that she has hatched take their first plunge into the mill-pond, and in spite of her clucking and pother sail off into the expanse of waters heedless of all remonstrance, we might be better able to sympathize with the worthy old servitor as his young master launched into ever new and more ambitious ventures. He survived his active faculties, and was an object of kindly care and liberality long after he had ceased even to deceive himself with the fancy that he could be of service in the business.

CHAPTER V.

HOPE PARK.

THE premises on the Castle Hill became ere long
too limited for the rapidly-growing business.
William Nelson had been joined in the enterprise by
his younger brother, Thomas; and with their combined energy many novel features were developed and
advances made in fresh avenues of trade. The publications of the establishment were attracting attention by
their improved typography and tasteful embellishment.
Ampler room and greater subdivision of labour had become indispensable. So, looking around for some more
suitable locality, their attention was directed to a group
of antiquated dwellings at the east end of the Meadows,
the remains of one of the suburban villages swallowed
up when Old Edinburgh burst its mural barriers and
extended over the surrounding heights.

In an address given by William Nelson to those in
his employment, at one of his social entertainments,
when a building was in progress at Hope Park which
he then assumed was to be the final addition to the

works, he traced the rise of the firm, interspersing the graver narrative with humorous incidents, and with kindly notices of some whom he referred to as faithful fellow-workers, from the time when he first gathered them around him in the new workrooms on the Castle Hill. One of the reminiscences of their entertainer's narrative is thus recalled:—When Hope Park grounds were about to be built upon, Mr. Nelson, being curious to explore the place, made a visit to what he described as a wilderness of cabbage gardens, with no end of pig-sties. One grumphy (Anglice, a sow) he noticed in a corner where the joiner's workshop afterwards stood, which, as he humorously described it, "kept its carriage!" The body of a four-wheeled coach, still in good condition, had been consigned to this novel use. The contrast was striking when, in later years, the smooth grass lawn, with its tasteful array of shrubs and flower-plots, filled the area enclosed on three sides by the Hope Park works.

But the full development of the establishment was the result of years of patient and steady progress, until it grew to proportions adequate for the varied departments embraced in the comprehensive scheme, with all its ingenious improvements in machinery for economizing labour. Its tall chimney showed from afar the scale on which its operations were carried on; though at a later date William Nelson realized very strongly

the injury to the amenities of the city, and the obstruc-
tion to the magnificent views of the surrounding landscape, occasioned by such adjuncts to its manufactories,
and laboured by precept and example to get rid of them.
In the later Parkside Works gas-engines are the sole
motive power, and their general introduction was advo-
cated by him as a substitute for the unsightly chimney
with its obscuring volumes of smoke.

With the numerous workmen that were ultimately
engaged in all the varied branches of skilled labour, the
Hope Park establishment came to be recognized as one
of the most important centres of economic industry in
the city; and, so far as printing, publishing, and binding are concerned, is spoken of by Mr. Bremner, in his
" Industries of Scotland," as the most extensive house
in Scotland.   The new buildings, when completed,
formed a stately range of offices enclosing three sides
of a square, where, under a well-organized division of
labour, with the aid of machinery adapted to its
varied operations, the entire work, from the setting of
the types to the issue of the bound and illustrated
volumes, was done on the premises.   Compositors,
draughtsmen, photographers, lithographers, steel, cop-
per, and wood engravers, electrotypers, stereotypers,
folders, stitchers, and binders, plied their industrious
skill.   The work-men and women employed on the
establishment latterly numbered nearly six hundred;

and few centres of industry have been characterized by more harmonious relations between the representatives of capital and labour.

The printing of books has constituted an important branch of Scottish industry from the days of Chepman and Miller, on through Bassendyne, Hart, and Symson, to our own time. The names of Fowlis, Constable, Ballantyne, Cadell, Blackwood, Oliver and Boyd, Chambers, Blackie, Collins, Neill, Black, and Nelson, are all familiarly associated with the literary history of the century; and, with only three exceptions, they belong to Edinburgh. It was fitting, indeed, that Edinburgh should take the lead in developing the typographer's art, where, in 1507, Walter Chepman set up the first printing-press in Scotland; and where, in the memorable year when "the flowers o' the forest were a' wede away" on Flodden Hill, he built the beautiful Chepman Aisle which still adorns the collegiate church of St. Giles, and endowed there a chaplainry at the altar of St. John the Evangelist. Edinburgh, in the days of the Scottish Caxton, was even more noteworthy for its authors than its typographers. Dunbar, Gawain Douglas, and the makers of that brilliant age, were followed by Montgomery, Drummond, Allan Ramsay, and Fergusson; and along with this array of poets, reaching to him whom Burns owned as his master, Hume, Robertson, Mackenzie, Adam Smith, Dugald Stewart, and Walter

Scott, combined to transform their old romantic town into the Modern Athens of later years. Their genius was not without its influence on the special aspect of Edinburgh's industries, including some of the novel forms of periodical literature which have so largely contributed to the culture of the masses.

The social entertainments and lectures provided by William Nelson at an early stage for his employés have already been noticed ; but in the spring of 1868 he extended his generous sympathy over an ampler field, and organized a *fête* for the whole journeymen printers and stereotypers of Edinburgh. The invitation met with a cordial response, and the appearance presented by the assembled guests in the galleries of the Museum of Science and Art was the theme of admiring comment. They were summoned to this novel social gathering by one who justly claimed recognition as an employer "who set a high value upon whatever is calculated to foster kindly feelings between man and man." The invitation said : "For one evening let us lay aside care or irksome duty, and come out with those we love best, and let us look each other fairly in the face. In the matter of head we do not much differ; at heart we are agreed. We need to have the bow unstrung occasionally. Let us do so in company for once, and see if we can help each other to a happy evening." The answer to this was the assembly of upwards of a thousand workmen, with their wives and sweethearts, in the Industrial Museum, to listen to a lecture by Mr. W. H. Davenport Adams, on the noble art in the service of which they were enlisted; and to enjoy the humour and pathos of some of Scotland's choicest national songs, including Burns's proud protest, which could there be appreciated without any thought of social wrong—" A man's a man for a' that!" The *Scottish Typographical Circular*, in its comments on this unique gathering, remarked: "Here were a thousand men, nearly all in superfine black coats and spotless shirt-fronts; a thousand women in tasteful dresses and bonnets of the latest mode, setting off the comely features of the printers' wives, or the fresh, pretty faces of their sweethearts; and in all this great mass of the 'lower orders' not a word out of joint; not a gesture of impatience; no crowding, jostling, or selfish preferring of one's own enjoyment; nothing but courtesy and that perfect good breeding which prompts men to give their neighbour's comfort the precedence of their own convenience." It was a gathering that Scotland might be proud of, whether we assign to the host or the guests the chief prominence. The matter of dress, to which the critic so specially directed attention, was not unworthy of note as an evidence of provident thrift, and of the self-respect which is nowhere more fitting than in the skilled artisan.

The spirit manifested in gatherings such as this is the best antidote for those conflicts between labour and capital which have proved so detrimental to both. Yet, as will be seen by a letter addressed less than four years later to his former traveller, Mr. James Campbell, he had evidence that a perfect solution of this great social problem has yet to be devised. The letter is dated from Dunkeld, where he had been spending a holiday with his family. In 1851 he had married Miss Catherine Inglis of Kirkmay, Crail; and at the date of the letter he was surrounded by a happy family, consisting of his son Frederick and four daughters, to whom he thus alludes: "The children have enjoyed their stay immensely, and none more than Master Fred, who got capital trout-fishing in the Braan, a tributary of the Tay, and in the Butterstone, a stream about six miles distant." His greatest happiness was in his own family circle, and surrounded by the friends whom he welcomed to his hospitable home. But the cares inseparable from his extensive commercial transactions could not always be so exorcised; and now a succession of inclement seasons and bad harvests was clouding the prospects of all. "We have had," he writes, "a most miserable time of it for many months past, as far as weather is concerned. I don't remember of such a long continuance of wet weather as there has been this year. It has lasted, I may almost say, all summer, up to within the last few days; and the result is that the crops have suffered terribly. As to the potatoes, the disease is everywhere, and potato starch-mills will have full employment this winter. It is a time calling for sympathy and forbearance on all hands. But, in addition, strikes for shorter hours and increase of wages are the order of the day; and it looks as if the words of the song, 'Hard times come again no more,' were ere long, as a general rule, not to be suitable for this country, as such times cannot be far distant for both masters and men, if there be not a cessation soon to this war between capital and labour. Things are all quiet at present in the trades of printing and bookbinding, but it is rumoured that heavy demands for both shorter hours and higher wages will be made by the men next month; and it is known that they have been preparing for a struggle by subscribing largely to a strike-fund ever since the beginning of the year, so that there is no doubt coming events are casting their shadows before.

"Things must be in a strange way in New York just now with operative printers. We know this from two of our men, who went out there some months ago in the hope of bettering their condition; but they were glad to come back to us, and they are both at work again, each at the machine at which he worked before he left. The history of the experiences of one of the men was as follows:—He got to New York, but he had no sooner begun to look out for work than he was set upon by a committee of operative printers, who were at the time on strike, and he was offered eleven dollars a week if he would not ask for work. The offer was too good a one for him to refuse, and he went about for several weeks with his hands in his pockets. By-and-by he was asked if he would not like to go back to Scotland. He said he had no objections, and it was arranged that his passage back should be paid. When the day came for his leaving, some of the New York men came down to the steamer to see him off, and they gave him five dollars for pocket-money during the voyage, and a sum of ten dollars to give to his wife, whom he had left behind in Edinburgh. And so he left the shores of America. The story of the other man is still more strange. He took work in an office in which there was a strike; but after being there for a week, he found his position so uncomfortable from annoyance from the men who had left, that he went and told his master he would have to leave on account of this. But what was his surprise when his master told him that he need not allow this state of matters to continue, as he had just to put a ball through one of the fellows, and there would be an end of it; and that the utmost that would be done to him in the way of punishment would be a day or two's confinement in the police office or jail. He then handed him a revolver and said, 'Take this and make good use of it, and you'll have a quiet life for the future.' This pistol I have now in my possession, and it is worth having as a curiosity."

At an earlier date the mischievous effects of a strike extended to the Hope Park works, ending in the places of some of the strikers being supplied by other applicants. But the victims learned by experience that they never appealed in vain to the sympathy of William Nelson, even when their share in the revolt had been characterized by ingratitude or breach of faith. It was sufficient that they were impoverished. "Poor fellow!" he would say, "he brought it on himself; but what of that?" And the liberal aid was given only too readily; for the plea was discovered to be one to which he most promptly responded, and was resorted to frequently by impostors who preyed on his kindly sympathy. What, indeed, the Rev. Dr. Alison remarked of him after his death, when he said: "He simply could not turn from distress of any sort without doing something to relieve it," was no more than an echo of the sentiment which experience had rendered familiar to many.

CHAPTER VI.

EGYPT AND PALESTINE.

THE excursions of early years, and the longer holiday rambles of student life, for which the environs of Edinburgh and the neighbouring shores of Fife afforded so many attractions, were exchanged for a time for the prosaic rounds of the commercial traveller and book-agent. But this duty was transferred ere long to trustworthy subordinates; and so soon as prosperity rewarded the intelligent labours of the young adventurer, the spirit that prompted earlier excursions revived. This was further stimulated by that keen desire to see and judge for himself in reference to all matters of general interest which manifested itself through life. The occurrence of any unusual event, or the opening up of some new region, was sufficient at any time to awaken the desire to explore a scene rendered interesting by its novelty, or by the exceptional circumstances which attracted his notice. When the first Pacific Railway was completed, he crossed the Atlantic in company with Mrs. Nelson, travelled to

San Francisco, visited the Yellowstone Region and the Mariposa Valley, and returned through Canada to renew his intercourse with old friends there. While in the Mariposa Valley, Mrs. Nelson was presented with one of the giant *Sequoia*, or *Wellingtonia*, which now bears, on a marble tablet attached to it, the name of "Auld Reekie," then bestowed on it. At Salt Lake City a Scotsman addressed Mr. Nelson by name, and begged him to convey his respects to his old clergyman, the Rev. W. Arnot of Edinburgh; but in mentioning this, Mr. Nelson dryly added that the Free Churchman of Salt Lake City seemed to take very kindly to its spiritual wives! He visited Paris in 1851, and exposed himself to its dangers at the time of the famous *coup d'état* by which the Third Napoleon made himself emperor. Twenty years later he hastened again to the French capital in the perilous outbreak of the Commune; and when the Christmas season of 1879 was overclouded by the disastrous fall of the Tay Bridge, immediately on learning of the event he made his way to Dundee to see for himself the ruins and to investigate the cause. He succeeded in finding a man who had watched the lights of the train as it swept on in the profound darkness, and was startled by their being suddenly extinguished. The bridge had given way; and the train, with all its passengers, was precipitated into the Tay. In like manner he set out for the Scilly Islands on the occasion of the wreck of the *Schiller ;* travelled to Ischia after the occurrence of the earthquake of 1881, in which the town of Casamicciola was almost totally destroyed ; and when, in the following year, the suspension of the Habeas Corpus Act led to a violent popular outbreak in Connemara, he crossed over to Ireland, that he might visit the disturbed district and judge for himself of the merits of the conflict.

The amount of preparation for even the longest journey was amazingly trifling. William Nelson would start almost at a day's notice for an extended tour ; and this course of procedure, so characteristic of his equanimity, conjoined with calm, resolute endurance, was curiously exemplified in his first extended journey. In 1849 he left home with the intention of spending a six weeks' holiday in the south of Europe. He was in Leghorn when a letter reached him which showed that all was going on satisfactorily in the business. He thereupon decided to make an extended journey to the East. But his funds were exhausted, and it was before the days of railways or telegraphs. With a faith in human nature characteristic of him through life, he stepped into the counting-house of Messrs. Henderson Brothers, the leading British merchants in Leghorn. He was a total stranger, with no introduction. He told them his story, and asked them to cash a draft on Edinburgh for

£300. They looked at him, and after a pause told him to draw the cheque, and gave him the money. The strangers became friends in later years; and one day, when Mr. Robert Henderson was dining at Salisbury Green, William Nelson asked him how it was that he and his brother had ventured to give a stranger so large a sum. "Well," said Mr. Henderson, "in plain truth, it was just your Scotch tongue and honest Scotch face, and nothing else!" The friendship which originated in this novel introduction lasted with their lives.

There was, in truth, something singularly winning in his open, handsome countenance; and its influence on strangers was anew illustrated at a later date, when Mrs. Nelson accompanied him in a tour through the Black Forest. They were overtaken by a thunderstorm when in Baden-Baden, and taking refuge in the nearest shop, they found it devoted to articles of *virtu*. A woman in charge, who spoke English fluently, received them courteously, and responded to Mr. Nelson's inquiries in a way that greatly interested him. On leaving he expressed his grateful thanks, and said he would have liked to make some purchases, but unfortunately his remaining funds were not more than sufficient for his journey home. The reply was: "Take whatever you please, sir. No one could look in your face and distrust you." He did accordingly carry off some choice objects of *virtu*, always a temptation to him; the money for which, it is scarcely necessary to add, was duly remitted on reaching England.

Provided, on such novel security, with funds requisite for a prolonged tour in the East, he was absent upwards of ten months, and turned the time to account with characteristic assiduity. The late President of Queen's College, Belfast, the Rev. Dr. J. Leslie Porter, who, as a traveller in Palestine, was familiar with the scenes embraced in Mr. Nelson's tour, and repeatedly conversed with him on points of mutual interest, remarks:—"He did not as a rule enter into detailed descriptions of the localities he had visited. His chief desire apparently was to elicit from those with whom he talked the fullest information, as if to add to or correct his own impressions. One thing particularly struck me: his questions were all pertinent and exactly to the point. He showed a talent in obtaining exactly the information he wished such as I have never known equalled, except in the case of one person. He could glean a wonderful amount of knowledge in a very brief period. He had himself been a close and accurate observer. He knew exactly the points which, from want of time or opportunity, he had not been able perfectly to grasp, and he put his questions in a form that brought out every particle of information the person he addressed could give.

"Of Damascus Mr. Nelson spoke with great enthusiasm. 'Yes,' he said, 'richness, beauty, and fertility are there. Where,' he asked, 'was the scene of Paul's conversion? Was it near the east gate, where tradition has located it?' I pointed out that this could scarcely be, as Paul was on his way from Jerusalem, and the road from the Holy City approaches Damascus from the opposite side. He next inquired whether there was still any tradition of Abraham; and he was very much interested when I told him that a few miles to the north there is still a shrine, at the foot of the hills, called the prayer-place of Abraham. 'Is not that,' he said, 'a proof of the tenacity with which even the oldest traditions cling to the country?' There was much in this; and he seemed to feel, as others have felt, that it may be used as an argument in favour of the truth of the early Christian traditions regarding the holy places of Jerusalem and other cities in Palestine. He asked much about the leprosy. 'Did any tradition of it exist in Damascus?' I remember well how deeply he seemed to be impressed when I told him that a short distance outside the east gate there were the remains of a very ancient building, called Naaman's House, and that a portion of it was still used as a leper hospital. He said to me, 'I looked for the Straight Street, mentioned in connection with the conversion of St. Paul, but could see no trace of it.' Then I told him

the results of more recent researches; how they had
brought to light the position and character of that
great street which ran through the city from the east
to the west gate, and had on each side a double row of
columns, fragments of which can still be seen in the
houses and courts adjoining."

But he had a no less keen eye for the modern
Damascus, with its motley population, its narrow
streets and thronged bazaars, all full of strange Eastern
life and habits. "The mean, dirty thoroughfares,
worse," as he says, "than an Old Town Edinburgh close,
run between low, shabby-looking houses; and nothing
surprised me more than when I was taken through a
long dark passage, to suddenly find that the shabby
street-front concealed a beautiful court, laid out in
garden fashion, with a fine fountain in the centre, and
flower-beds and orange trees, and round this the
chambers, brightly furnished with cushions and mat-
ting, etc., all opening on to it, like a scene from the
Arabian Nights' Entertainments." Nevertheless the
predominant thought in his mind was the Damascus
of Roman and New Testament times; the city to
which Saul the persecutor was journeying when he
was arrested on the way, and commissioned to go far
hence to proclaim the gospel of glad tidings to the
Gentile world.

Having gratified his intelligent curiosity, in seeking to discover the ancient localities of Damascus associated with Scripture history, he proceeded by way of Lebanon to Jerusalem. The associations of the city of Zion, of Nazareth, the Jordan, the Syrian desert, and the Dead Sea, were replete with interest to a mind trained from earliest childhood in devout familiarity with every incident of sacred story. The novel scenes of Eastern life were, moreover, explored with peculiar zest in this his first escape from the restraints of homely Western civilization into that strange old East where the customs and ideas of an ancient past still survive. In referring to this visit to Jerusalem he remarks:—" I was there before any guide-book was written; and so I had to consult my Bible, and occasionally Josephus, on a point of history. After these I found Robinson's 'Biblical Researches' the most thorough and useful. Robinson seemed to me to write, and study, and investigate as a scholar. Perhaps he paid rather too little regard to tradition; but this was natural in a place like Jerusalem, which absolutely swarms with the most absurd legends. He lays down on the whole a firm basis of biblical and historical facts; then he leads one on in a logical and critical manner to the truth regarding the exact sites of the great events of the Gospel narrative: the site of the Temple, of the Palace of David, of the Hall of Judgment in which Pilate sat, of the old walls and gates of the

Holy City, etc. Then Robinson seemed to me to prove that the Holy Sepulchre could not have been where it is now located."

The controverted questions about the topography of Jerusalem, which have since received such abundant elucidation, were all familiar to him, and were discussed with keenest interest when he met with any one who had either visited the sacred city, or made its historical details a subject of research. The scenes of the nativity, the crucifixion, and the holy sepulchre, of the agony in the garden, and the ascension, were all investigated by him with critical care. Dr. Porter furnishes the following memoranda of their conversation on those subjects :—

"He asked me my views as to the true site of Calvary. Was I convinced that it was not—or, as Robinson affirms, could not have been—within the compass of the present walls ? If not, then where was it ? He several times said, as if by way of suggestion, that it was either on the north side of the modern city, or to the east, on the brow of the Kidron Valley. 'Did you ever consider,' he asked me, 'the statement of the evangelist to the effect that the women, as if afraid to approach, viewed the awful tragedy from afar?' He was pleased when I suggested that possibly the true site of Calvary was not far south of St. Stephen's Gate, where two public roads passed a short distance off—

one leading north to Samaria and Galilee, the other east, over the Kidron and Olivet, to Jericho and the Jordan. 'Yes,' he said; 'and the women would then have a clear view of the whole scene, from a safe distance, on the side of the Mount of Olives, beyond the deep and narrow valley.'"

To this succeeded discussions on the value of the local traditions in reference to the scenes latterly associated with so much superstition and deceit; and the possibility of identifying them with the help of local topography and the sacred narrative. "'Where,' he asked me, 'would you locate the scene of the ascension? Was it, or could it have been, on the traditional spot at the Church of the Ascension on the summit of Olivet? If you adopt this tradition, then how,' he asked, 'do you explain the words of the evangelist: "He led them out as far as to Bethany"?' My reply was, 'I do not admit the reality of the traditional site.' He said this impressed himself very deeply when he crossed over the Mount of Olives to Bethany. He felt convinced that the scene of that wonderful last interview with the disciples was some spot near the village. 'I think,' he said, 'our Lord took the disciples to a retired place, not in view either of Jerusalem or of the village of Bethany. Then,' he added thoughtfully, 'was there not some analogy between this scene and that of the transfiguration on a high mountain apart?

Would not the solitude impress the disciples more forcibly with the glory of the appearance of the angels, and of his own close and immediate intercourse with the hosts of heaven?' The thoughtfulness and depth of many of Mr. Nelson's remarks upon the events of the life and death of Jesus often struck me. His visit to Palestine was brief; but he grasped in a very short time the most interesting and important points, and he connected them, with a kind of intuitive readiness and accuracy, with the events of the sacred narrative. He spoke on several occasions of the noble and yet very peculiar site of the Holy City, different in many respects from his previous ideas; but the moment he saw it, more deeply fixing in his mind the truth of the Psalmist's words: 'Beautiful for situation is Mount Zion.' The view from the top of Olivet, and that from the old road which winds round and along its side from Bethany, was, he told me, to him by far the most instructive. 'I read,' he said, 'the words of Jesus, when he looked on and wept over the city, with a feeling of their reality and wonderful vividness such as I had never experienced before.' Another thing he observed more than once: 'I was disappointed in the scenery of Palestine. I did not see, and I could not fully understand, the glowing descriptions in some parts of Scripture of its fertility and beauty. When I thought of England and Scotland, and compared their fertile lowlands and magnificent highlands with the bare plains and rocky hills of Judah, I felt much difficulty in divesting my mind of the idea that even the sacred writers indulged in exaggeration. But,' he added, 'I suppose my Western ideas were entirely different from theirs as to what are the elements of richness and grandeur.' I reminded him of the words of Scripture : 'A land of corn and wine and oil olive.' 'Yes,' he said; 'most probably an Eastern would despise even the best parts of Scotland because they want the vines and the olives.' "

The experiences of this visit to the sacred scenes of Bible story left an enduring impression on William Nelson's mind; and their special character in association with his own early training justify some detail in reference to researches otherwise only possessed of personal interest. As a traveller, he made no pretension to geographical exploration or scientific research ; and unless when in company with one from whom he could derive information, he rarely referred to his experiences while abroad. His longest journeys were regarded by himself as only extended holiday rambles. But they were carried out with characteristic zeal; and some of the incidents which may be gleaned from them have their biographical value in so far as they disclose traits of personal character. He made his way by the desert route from Palestine to

Egypt, where he spent his Christmas in Grand Cairo, and commenced the ascent of the Nile early in the following January. His fellow-traveller in the latter country, Major MacEnery, furnishes some interesting reminiscences of their voyage up the Nile. " I preserve a lively memory," he writes, " of the unvarying geniality of our companion, and of his spirit of exploration. In this respect he was truly remarkable ; indefatigable in the pursuit of information concerning even the minutest object of interest within reach ; never satisfied without a personal inspection, when at all possible ; neither hunger, thirst, nor fatigue deterring him from the gratification of being able to say conscientiously, ' I have seen it.' "

The impressions left on the traveller's mind by the scenes of special interest in the Holy Land, and some of the incidents which their memory recalled, were a frequent source of pleasure to his friends in after years. Some of them indeed enjoyed more tangible memorials, in the shape of inscribed tablets of the wood of the Mount of Olives ; a carved memento of the Dead Sea fashioned from its black volcanic rock ; a gold shekel, —subsequently deposited by Mr. James Campbell in the Presbyterian Theological College at Montreal,—and other like gifts. Nor were the attractions of the land of the Pharaohs less keenly appreciated. It had its ancient memories, both sacred and profane, alike inter-

esting to the intelligent explorer. There were the
works of Pharaohs of older centuries than Moses or
Joseph; the walls of Abu-Simbul, graven by the son
of Theokles with their Hellenic record centuries before
the Father of History began his task; the Thebes of
the Hundred Gates, with its magnificent ruins authen-
ticating Homer's verse; and Ptolemaic and Roman
remains, modern by comparison. For all this the
traveller's early training had unconsciously prepared
him; and every feature was calculated to revive the
archæological tastes which found so many votaries
among the members of the "Juvenile Literary Society."
He ascended the Nile to the Second Cataract, and
gleaned some choice antiques from the relics with
which the poor fellaheen tempt the traveller in that
cradle-land of the world's civilization. Those included
Osirian figures bearing hieroglyphic inscriptions, one
especially with the cartouch of an early Pharaoh; a
brick from Thebes, stamped with the cartouch of
Thothmes III.; a porcelain stamp similarly inscribed;
and other prized memorials. Above all, he had gazed
with delight on the monuments of a long-vanished
civilization, and explored with curious interest scenes
associated with the Bible stories learned by him at his
mother's knee. His inquisitive research was constantly
on the alert, and the same thorough-going energy
characterized him as a traveller and a man of business.

But along with all this, one exceptional trait may be noted, eminently characteristic of the man. A letter addressed to him from Cairo by Abdallah, his old Egyptian dragoman, which reached Edinburgh soon after his death, recalled the fact that his faithful servitor had been the annual recipient of a kindly remittance through all the years since they voyaged together up the Nile. Abdallah writes with a borrowed pen: "I have received your kind letter with the five pounds, and was very happy to hear that you are in perfect health, with your dearest family and with your friends. I always think of you, and beg God to be with you and spare you. All my friends are very thankful for your great kindness to me. I hope some day some gentleman of your friends come I shall have the honour to serve him." For his remembrance of the faithful dragoman had been practically shown, not only by pecuniary remittances, but also by recommending him to other travellers, until poor Abdallah's creditors pounced upon the baggage of Dr. Henry Field, to whose service he had been commended, and so his prospects as a dragoman were ruined. In writing to Major MacEnery in May 1886, Mr. Nelson says: "I had a letter not long ago from poor old Abdallah. It was just the old story of his being unable to do anything in the way of earning a livelihood. He sent me a letter addressed to the Lord

Mare of London, an old fellow-traveller in the Holy Land, which I duly delivered to his lordship; but he did not take the hint and give me something for the poor dragoman."

The experiences of the traveller were occasionally turned to account in unexpected ways in after years, when dealing with his own workpeople. One instance was recalled in an address, already referred to, delivered at Parkside soon after his death. On the introduction of a greatly improved sewing-machine at Hope Park much opposition was excited among the girls, who unanimously protested in favour of the old-fashioned, familiar instrument. Thereupon Mr. Nelson humorously told them that they reminded him of the difficulties among the Arabs engaged in digging the Suez Canal. They had at first scooped out the sand into baskets, which they carried on their heads, and so transported the soil to the new embankments. This process was much too slow for the contractors, who accordingly provided them with shovels and wheelbarrows. But when the latter were filled, the Arabs could not be persuaded to trundle them in the ordinary way, but hoisted the wheel-barrows on their heads, and so trudged along to the place of deposit!

The unfamiliar scenes and incidents of Eastern life, both in Egypt and Palestine, had made a deep impression on William Nelson's mind, and were frequently recalled. The letter to Major MacEnery, his old fel-low-voyager on the Nile, in which he refers to his dragoman, Abdallah, was written at a time when the first news of the troubles in the Soudan was awaken-ing attention at home; and, recalling his old experi-ences, he remarks: "How strange it is that the Arabs in the Soudan should be troubling our troops there at Koshi, our most advanced post from Wady Halfi. I was under the impression that it would have been impossible for them to have advanced in anything like a formidable body so far north. But those wild sons of the desert can live almost upon air, and go about like clouds of locusts; and as they are not troubled with artillery or other impediments, they may cause us some trouble, more especially as they are animated with fanatical zeal against the infidels, and they do not know when they are beaten."

The traveller brought back with him a duly attested document bearing the seal of the Holy Sepulchre (a cross potence and crosslets), furnished to Gulielmus Nelson by the prior of the Latin convent in Jerusalem, in his quality of guardian of the Holy Sepulchre, at-testing that he had in an edifying spirit visited the sacred places around the Holy City; and had indeed conformed to the requirements of a devout pilgrim to an extent which, if literally true, would have been in strange antagonism to all his early training. For the veracious prior of the Convent of St. Salvator certifies over his official seal that the aforesaid Gulielmus Nelson had not only visited the principal sanctuaries, but that "with great devotion he had heard mass in them all"!

A more genuine reminiscence of travel, with which the pilgrim surprised his friends, was the novel feature of a fine black beard, the imposing effect of which probably had its share in the opinion formed by the Syrian peasants that he was a learned leech. Commenting long after on the reputed virtues of some much-vaunted pills, he said they were no doubt as efficacious as those he used to make in Palestine. The villagers flocked to his tent, importuning him and his companions for medicine. With much gravity he distributed among them the pills he had fashioned out of the spare breakfast loaf; and, with the faith of the recipients in his prescriptions, supplemented as they doubtless were in cases of actual suffering by a liberal *backshish*, he had no doubt that he effected as many cures as some of the patent-medicine vendors. As to the black beard, the custom in that respect has so entirely changed since then that it is difficult for the present generation to realize the astonishment which the strange appendage excited. To some grave elders it almost appeared as if he had literally cast in his lot with the followers of the false prophet. The idea of even a moustache as the possible appendage of a civilian first dawned on the English mind when Prince Albert set the fashion in society. But this innovation was viewed with suspicion among all sober denizens of the mart. As to the wearing of a beard, it would have been sufficient to ruin the credit of the most reputable trader. There is a report in "The Dial," from the pen of Emerson, of a grand convention of enthusiasts held at Boston a few years before. "If," says he, "the assembly was disorderly, it was picturesque. Mad men, mad women, *men with beards*, Dunkers, Muggeltonians, Come-outers!"—and so the enumeration of the eccentric medley proceeds. The beard, as is obvious, was an innovation beyond all tolerance. But the art of photography, in its earlier form of ambrotype, was in vogue. The traveller accordingly had his portrait taken in his Eastern dress, with moustache, beard, and long pipe. Some time after, when showing to a friend the relics he had brought from the East, he produced along with them the portrait, and asked what he thought of the Egyptian pasha. To his extreme amusement, his friend exclaimed, "What a bloodthirsty look that fellow has in his face!"

It is abundantly manifest that at that date, whatever might be thought of the beard, it could not be worn in the Hope Park counting-house during business hours. Before, however, its sacrifice to the prudery of that decorous, clean-shaven generation, a party of old schoolmates, of whom the present writer was one, assembled at his dinner-table. The host received us in the flowing robes of an Arab sheik; and with his turban and fine beard, looked as though he might have sat with Abraham at the tent door. In the course of the evening a tempting-looking bottle was produced, with the announcement that it had been brought from the Holy Land; and this he commended so zealously as to put some of the knowing ones on the alert. Each filled his glass as the bottle passed round, took a sip, and then watched its progress; till a rash young toper swallowed the major contents of his glass at a gulp, and then, amid roars of laughter, began coughing, sputtering, and anathematizing the potation. For the seductive bottle was filled with water brought by our host from the Dead Sea: a sulphureous, briny draught fit only for the revellers of Gomorrah.

The enduring impressions left on the mind of William Nelson by his visit to the Holy Land found expression, in long subsequent years, in a well-known work, "The Land and the Book," which in its final form embraced: 1. Palestine and Jerusalem; 2. Lebanon, Damascus, and Beyond the Jordan; and 3. Central Palestine and Phœnicia. The Rev. W. M. Thomson was commissioned to explore the sacred scenes of Bible story, with a view to the production of a work that should furnish for others somewhat of the vivid realizations that William Nelson had experienced in his own visit to the land

> " Over whose acres walked those blessed feet
> That eighteen hundred years ago were nailed
> For our redemption to the bitter cross."

The following extract from a letter written in July 1880 to his old schoolfellow, Dr. Simpson, refers to the volume as then in progress, and to the perils from which the manuscript had been so unexpectedly rescued :—

" We are not out yet with the new volume of ' The Land and the Book,' and I do not expect that it will be ready for publication before the middle of next month. It is a truly superb work, and it has been got up regardless of expense. It will, when completed, form three volumes. Strange to say, the manuscript of one of them, ' Egypt, Mount Sinai, and the Desert,' turned up the other day after we had given it up as having been destroyed at our great fire, with many other valuable manuscripts. But, fortunately, it was in one of the drawers of a writing-desk which had escaped the devouring flames, and the manuscript was discovered quite unexpectedly, after the author had for a long time been informed of the loss that had been sustained."

CHAPTER VII.

CHURCH—MARRIAGE.

THE year 1843 is a memorable one in Scottish history. The controversy between the two parties into which the National Church was divided had been concentrated for years on the old question of patronage, or the right of the people to the free choice of their clergymen. Under the leadership of Dr. Chalmers, in co-operation with an able body of clergy and laymen, enactments were passed by the Church courts restoring to the people their rights in the choice of pastors. Influential patrons acquiesced in its operation, and the sanguine hope was entertained that a peaceful solution of the grievance which had long been a source of bitterness had at length been arrived at. But in the famous Auchterarder case the civil courts were appealed to; the action of the General Assembly, the supreme court of the Church, was overruled; and on the 18th of May 1843 four hundred and seventy-four ministers of the Church of Scotland voluntarily re-signed their livings, and cast themselves on the liberality of their people. Ten years of conflict, marked with an ever-increasing intensity of feeling, and with all the inevitable fruits of embittered controversy, had ended in the disruption of the National Church. It was an event without a parallel since the ejection from their benefices of upwards of two thousand ministers of the English National Church in 1662 by the Act of Uniformity.

It is difficult for the present generation to fully estimate the feeling which the Disruption called forth, or the bitter antagonism which in many cases it engendered. The early training and all the strong personal convictions of William Nelson alike determined his sympathy with what claimed to be "The Free Church of Scotland." The movement which led to this result had appeared to him, as to others, to furnish a practical solution of the difficulties which held his Covenanting fathers aloof from the National Church. The financial question was an important one, and long continued to be so; for not only churches but colleges had to be built, theological professorships to be endowed, poor congregations to be sustained, and the foreign mission field provided for. In all this work William Nelson was a generous co-operator; and to the close of his life he continued to respond with unstinted liberality to all the claims which it involved. His brother John, who became the esteemed pastor of

the Free West Church of Greenock, was referred to
after his premature death, in an eloquent tribute by
Professor Blaikie, as "one whose natural gifts were of
a high order, and whose early position as a student was
most distinguished. He was known to be of far too
independent a nature to fall into any line merely because it was traditional or conventionally proper. He
had courage and capacity to strike out for himself;
and he had spent much time in study in Germany at
a time when few students went thither, and when such
a course was regarded as somewhat suspicious." The
old Covenanting blood was in his veins; but he had
hoped that the National Church was resuming its
fidelity to the faith of his fathers, when the Disruption
came, and he cast in his lot with the champions of
freedom. Personal sympathy, therefore, as well as
strong convictions, enlisted William Nelson on the side
of the Free Church; but he never was a partisan. No
trace of bitterness sullied the earnest zeal with which
he promoted the cause that he had at heart. His convictions were clear, and his devotion to the Church
unwavering; but this was never allowed to interfere
with his personal relations to those who adhered to the
Established Church, nor with his response to appeals
made by them to his liberality. The testimony to this
effect was freely given when his death recalled the
incidents of earlier years. Among memoranda fur-

nished to me by Mr. John Miller of Glasgow is the
following note: "My sole companion in the railway
carriage on my return to Glasgow, after attending Mr.
Nelson's funeral, was a stranger, a clergyman of the
Established Church, who had travelled to Edinburgh
on the same melancholy errand. In conversation I
learned that Mr. Nelson and another to whom he referred had been friends of his from their earliest years.
But at the Disruption they both became members of
the Free Church. Thereupon, as the clergyman said,
his unnamed friend took umbrage at him for remaining
in the Established Church, and their friendship ceased.
It is not easy now to understand the bitterness of
feeling that existed at that time between those who
took different views on the question of the relation
between Church and State; but as regards Mr. Nelson,
such was his breadth of mind and catholic spirit, it
never made the slightest change on their friendship
through all the intervening years, and he spoke of
him 'as the best of all good men he had known.'"

But his broad-minded charity was in no degree
traceable to latitudinarian indifference. His convictions were strong, and when occasion required it, were
maintained with firmness, and defended with incisive
keenness of argument. And here it may be well to
note a characteristic trait. Few men were ever more
notably marked by transparent sincerity and truthful-

ness. If a truth told against his cause, it never occurred to him to withhold it. There was indeed an
amusing simplicity in the manner in which he would
disclose a fact seeming to reflect on his own party or on
himself; or, when in company with persons disposed to
arrogate to themselves rank or social position, he would
recall some homely incident or experience of his own
early life. But the same instinctive love of truth made
him intolerant of cant, or of any evasion in reference
to matters of faith. If he were perplexed with doubts,
as he often was, in reference to the modern conflict
between science and revelation, he would give abrupt
utterance to them in the most orthodox circles; and if
any attempt were made to evade or gloss over the
difficulty, his blunt reassertion of the point at issue, in
all its literal nakedness, was at times misunderstood
and even bitterly resented. Sanctimonious hypocrisy,
or anything savouring of insincerity in religion, was
abhorrent to his nature, and provoked his keenest
ridicule. For his sense of humour was great, and he
would expose pretentious inconsistencies in their most
ludicrous aspect, giving no little offence at times to
clerical offenders. To this habit of giving expression
of his convictions with all unguarded sincerity is, no
doubt, to be ascribed the remark in a letter of one of
his oldest Christian friends, when bearing testimony to
the earnestness with which in his last illness " he gave

proof that he had attained by God's help to true faith in the Son of God, and was conscious of having definitely accepted him as his personal Saviour, and given himself over to him on the warrant of God's own word of invitation." The writer, a devoted clergyman of the Free Church, adds: "There was an entire absence of the old levity, which you will remember used sometimes almost to shock and sadden even his best friends."

It was perhaps a want of tact,—a diplomatic element apt at times to verge on insincerity in which he was certainly deficient,—that led to his being so misjudged. But the same unconscious indifference to the prejudices of others could be seen when, among strangers at a public hotel or on the ocean, he would ask a blessing before dinner with the same earnest reverence as at his own table. The impression which his manner of saying grace produced on a stranger is thus expressed in a letter from an English lady, who, after his death, recalled the memories of more than one sojourn under his hospitable roof: "One always felt cheered in his presence by the glow of his great heart and that sweet genial kindness to all which was like sunshine in the room. I also greatly admired that dislike of any praise of himself which one always saw in him, and which is so rare......I so well remember in the Philiphaugh drawing-room before dinner his kindly talk to

us all, and his almost boyish fun : so interested in every
one, and saying playful things to me about palmistry,
etc.   But when we went in to dinner, I was always
struck with his unusual way of saying grace : the
reverence that came over him, as if he were actually
speaking to God, and as though from his heart he
was simply grateful day by day for each gift of the
heavenly Father.   I can almost hear again as I
write the rich deep tones of his voice as he asked the
blessing, and prayed that God would graciously take
away all our sins.   I have never heard a clergyman,
or any other person, who so impressed me with reverence and reality in saying grace as he did."   This
feeling was by no means singular.   In a letter from
Professor T. Grainger Stewart, a similar reference
occurs to "his mode of asking a blessing."   Alluding
to his wife, Professor Stewart says : " We were both
greatly impressed with the earnestness and reverence
with which he spoke, and on our way home talked of
it to one another."

To one in whom the influences of early training had
thus been confirmed by the personal convictions of
later years, the responsibilities of his influence as a
publisher were keenly realized.   The system which
he developed was based on the anticipated sale of
large editions at low prices.   Hence an important class
of works issued by some eminent publishing houses in

costly editions of from eight to twelve hundred copies lay entirely beyond the range of his publications. But the imprint of Thomas Nelson and Sons became ere long the guarantee for a pure, high-toned literature, admirably adapted for the special requirements of the school library and the home circle; and as success crowned the system of large and cheap editions, works of more permanent value were issued on the same plan.

The uniformity of the testimony to his integrity and business capacity borne by many whose relations with him were widely dissimilar removes all idea of exaggeration; while the terms in which they write of him are so diverse from the ordinary commendations of the mart or the exchange, as to show in a striking manner the influence exercised by an altogether exceptional character in the ordinary relations of business. Mr. Robertson, who was long his manager in New York, thus writes: "During the many years I had the privilege of knowing Mr. Nelson, I was increasingly drawn towards him by his strict integrity, his kindliness, his splendid energy, his intellectual activity, and his unostentatious piety. There was no duty so humble that he would not stoop to perform it; there was no amount of hard work or fatigue that ever turned him away from his purpose. There was no appeal ever made to him by the suffering or poverty-stricken that did not meet with a kindly and sympathetic response.

There was in him a fine appreciation of merit, regardless of the social status of its possessor; and although he would have been unwilling to admit it, there was in him a Christ-like going about continually doing good which was simply beautiful." This affectionate respect which he awakened in all who were brought into intimate relations with him as his trusted agents is constantly apparent. His confidence when once secured was implicit; and any breach of trust or neglect of duty was a source of intense pain to him, wholly apart from any idea of personal loss.

The following characteristic reminiscences are derived from notes furnished by Mr. John Miller, whose business transactions with Mr. Nelson, as a large paper manufacturer, brought them into frequent intercourse: "Mr. Nelson had an immense aptitude for the despatch of business, and great promptness of decision, never wasting any time talking over bargains. When a papermaker called and showed him a sample, if it was not to his mind, or the price too high, he would in the most courteous manner thank him for the sample, but he would in no way depreciate the paper. If the paper was right, he would say, 'Well, it is just the price we are paying;' or if the price were better, he would frankly say, 'It is a little better than the price we are buying at. I shall give you an order; and if you can maintain the quality at the price, we shall continue to order from you.' There was never any second bargain at settlement. If the paper sent was not according to sample, it would be paid for without remark, and no further orders given. Mr. Nelson had no time and no disposition to haggle over a bargain, and no man could better appreciate value. He was in every respect a very capable man of business. After his marriage he began to take business a little more leisurely; at all events, he seemed to take more time for the little courtesies of life, which were so greatly developed in his after years."

He had proved himself a true captain of industry; organized his extensive business on the most systematic basis; gathered around him a body of skilled and trusty workmen, on whose loyal co-operation he could rely; and having thus, with prudent foresight, surmounted the many impediments that had inevitably beset his way, he turned aside from the anxieties of business to make for himself a home, in which all the congenial elements of a singularly emotional and sensitive nature should thenceforth find free scope for development. He retained to the close of his life his interest in the multitudinous details of the printing and publishing works; but he found time for the gratification of many refined tastes, and for a practical sympathy in public questions, as well as in the exercise of an open-handed beneficence, the full extent of which has only been revealed since his death.

The new life of which marriage is the source began for William Nelson when he was in his thirty-sixth year. On the 24th of July 1851, Catherine Inglis, the daughter of Robert Inglis, Esquire of Kirkmay, Fife-shire, a descendant of Sir James Inglis, Bart., of Cramond, gave her hand, with her heart in it, to William Nelson. The marriage took place at the old mansion of Kirkmay, acquired by her father, with the estates of Sypsis and Kirkmay, on his return from a highly successful career in India. The maternal grandfather of the bride had seen long service there; and letters preserved by the family show that he was held in high esteem by Lord Cornwallis, and was the trusted and confidential friend of Warren Hastings. One of them, addressed to him while he was Resident at the Court of Scindia, is an amusing example of epistolary conciseness in preferring an unusual request; and as such was peculiarly germane to William Nelson's tastes, as well as to his sense of humour. His fondness for animals manifested itself at times in odd ways, and had he received any encouragement the pleasure grounds at Salisbury Green would have been apt to assume the character of a zoological garden. When travelling in California in 1870, along with Mrs. Nelson, he was reluctantly dissuaded from bringing off with him as a novel pet a "gofer," or beautifully striped species of lizard, which an Indian offered for sale. Here was a still more unmanageable pet in request by the old Indian viceroy in his letter to the grandfather of the bride :—

"BENARES, *14th March, 1784.*

"DEAR SIR,—If you can possibly contrive to procure for me a young lion of a size which may be carried over rocky and mountainous roads, I shall be much obliged to you. I want to gratify the eager desire which has been expressed by the ruler of Tibet to have one in his possession; the people of this country having a religious veneration for a lion, of which they know nothing but in the doubtful and fabulous relations of their own books.—I am, dear sir, yours affectionately,

"WARREN HASTINGS.

"To Lieutenant James Anderson."

But this ancestral reminiscence carries us far afield from the wedding-party at Kirkmay House, where the bride was given away by her brother, who had then succeeded to the estate; and so the old home was exchanged for one which she gladdened through all the happy years till that inevitable parting which every wedded union involves. Thenceforth life had for William Nelson a deeper meaning, and was passed in the quiet centre of a sunlight all his own, till he reached beyond the limit of the threescore years and ten.

The biographer must ever feel that he executes a delicate trust in drawing aside the curtain that veils the sanctities of home life. But here there was nothing to conceal. A friend who met Mr. and Mrs. Nelson at a German spa twenty years later thus writes: "I was greatly interested in watching him as he, with all the attention and devotion of a lover, refilled and carried the glass of water to his wife, and tended on her, then an invalid, with untiring care." And so it continued to be to the close. Thirty-six years of happy wedded union glided by. Daughters in time followed their mother's example, and left the old home to make new centres of happiness. Eveline, the eldest, was married in 1874 to Professor Annandale, Professor of Surgery in the University of Edinburgh; and in 1886 her sister Florence became the wife of S. Fraser MacLeod, Esquire, barrister, London, a friend of the family from early boyhood. By-and-by the little grandchildren presented themselves to claim their mothers' places in the hearts of those who had found it hard to reconcile themselves to the blanks round the old hearth, where Meta and Alice still remained, with their brother Frederick, to play the new *rôle* of uncle and aunts. The home of the Nelsons at Salisbury Green was familiar to many through all those years as a rare centre of genial hospitality, with some unique features of its own worthy of further note.

CHAPTER VIII.

SALISBURY GREEN.

THE unique site of the Scottish capital, embosomed in hills and looking out upon the sea, furnishes many charming nooks for suburban residence to its denizens; but among such the Nelsons' home stood in some respects unrivalled. Salisbury Green, a jointure house of the Prestonfield family, when purchased in 1770 by Lady Dick Cunningham, had, according to the traditions of the family, a ghost as its sole tenant; and notwithstanding the genial hospitalities, and all the brightness and beauty of its home-life in later years, the venerable ghost, a lady of grim visage, in antique coif and farthingale, continued to flit at rare intervals about her old haunts, and drew the curtains of fair young dreamers who had invaded her precincts. It was a plain old-fashioned house, though already graced with some of the undesigned picturesqueness due to additions of various dates, when William Nelson acquired the property in 1860. But, with his keen eye for beauty, he discerned at once the capabilities of the place, embosomed in stately trees, and commanding a view of almost unmatched grandeur and beauty.

Under his tasteful care, the old house was renovated, assuming externally the picturesque features of the domestic architecture of Scotland in the sixteenth century; and in accordance with the practice of the age of the Reformation, he carved round the entablature this apt motto, from the third chapter of Hebrews, " EVERY HOUSE IS BUILDED BY SOME MAN ; BUT HE THAT BUILT ALL THINGS IS GOD." Internally the drawing-room, an addition of its earlier proprietors, was a reproduction, in style and proportions, of that of Barley Wood, the charming abode of the amiable and gifted Hannah More. The house, so familiar to many strangers from other lands as well as to the citizens of Edinburgh, by reason of its hospitalities, was enriched in later years, by the accumulated acquisitions of its owner, with choice works of art and *virtu*, and especially with a valuable collection of bronzes and antique ceramic ware, not displayed for purposes of show, but scattered over the mantel-shelves and cabinets, or disposed about in every available nook and corner of the old house, as natural and fitting adjuncts of the tasteful owner's home.

But the unique charm of Salisbury Green as a city dwelling lies in its natural surroundings. The terraced lawn slopes to the east, and commands a historic land-

scape of rare beauty. The couchant lion of Arthur
Seat, a mountain in miniature, rises on the left in a
succession of bold cliffs and grassy slopes to a height of
eight hundred feet. The basaltic columns of Samson's
Ribs form a singularly bold feature at its base. On the
right, the rich undulating landscape terminates in an
insulated rock crowned with the picturesque ruin of
Craigmillar Castle, famous in Scottish history in the
days of the Jameses and Mary Stuart. Right below,
Duddingston Loch forms the central feature, with the
old village churchyard beyond. Under its mouldering
heaps the rude forefathers of many a generation lie
around the venerable parish church. Though defaced
by tasteless modern additions, the church still retains
the richly-moulded Norman chancel arch and south
doorway, the work of the same builders who reared the
Abbey of Holyrood in the time of David I.; while
away in the distant landscape are North Berwick Law,
Aberlady Bay, the Bass Rock, and beyond the Firth of
Forth the Fifeshire hills. The sudden transition from
the dust and bustle of the Dalkeith Road to the garden
terrace and the unique landscape beyond, never failed
to excite admiring wonder in the visitor who saw it for
the first time. It includes such a variety of attractive
features, and differs so greatly from anything usually
visible from the windows or garden-terrace of a city
dwelling, that even the most unimpressible yielded to

some sense of surprise.　Many a hearty tribute has accordingly been paid to its beauty.　The French artist, Gustave Doré, was charmed with the magnificent panorama; J. J. Hayes, the Arctic explorer, and Bayard Taylor, familiar as a traveller with the beauties of many lands, owned its attractions as exceptionally rare; and the expression of quiet delight with which Augustus Hare—fortunate in an unusually warm, bright day of early summer—lingered over every detail of the historic landscape, has left a vivid impression on the minds of those who recall the incidents of his visit. It was no show-place for strangers, for few men shrank with more instinctive reserve than William Nelson from anything savouring of display; but to friends and friends' friends it was ever accessible.　An American visitor, who, like so many others from beyond the Atlantic, received a hospitable welcome at Salisbury Green, thus recalls the place and its owner:—"I shall never forget the greeting that made us all so much at home, the gentle humour of our host at table, and then the quiet saunter in the summer evening in the garden; Samson's Ribs, a most curious geological formation, and the hill beyond reflecting the setting sun, on one of those long summer evenings we know nothing of in America.　Mr. Nelson pointed out a ruined castle where Queen Mary resided, and a rock out in the sea that had been a prison of the Covenanters.　Alto-

gether the scene and its pleasant associations are un-
forgetable."

Here, in this bright home, William Nelson dwelt,
surrounded by wife and children, with an ever-wel-
come circle of friends; and also with other objects of
his kindly consideration—his pet cockatoo, his peacocks,
his children's rabbits, etc., for his sympathetic nature
displayed itself strongly in his love for the lower animals. His favourite dogs made him subservient to
their caprices, for he could not bear to see an animal
neglected. The birds that frequented Salisbury Green
were a source of constant delight, and any injury done
to them excited his pity. He mourned over the disappearance of the larks, after a succession of wet seasons, as a personal loss; and an ill-timed jest about lark-
pies seemed to give him acute pain. The reappearance
of the birds in the spring, and their pairing and building, were a source of ever-renewed pleasure. But no
one entered more heartily into the humorous aspect of
things, even when the laugh was at his own expense;
and an occasion of this kind transpired during one of
my later visits to Salisbury Green. He had been
greatly charmed by the appearance of a pair of herons
that remained day after day stalking about the lawn,
wading in the pond, and seemingly well contented
to make themselves at home in the grounds. The
household was warned not to disturb the graceful

strangers; but after a time they disappeared, and then some stray fish-bones on the margin of the pond revealed the secret of their visit. They had only left when the last of its gold-fish had been disposed of!

The tenderness of William Nelson for the lower animals was shown in many ways. A companion of his boyhood recalls an incident of those early years. A party of boys at Kinghorn were off in a boat. They had obtained the prized loan of a gun, and each in his turn was to have a shot at the sea-gulls. William eagerly waited his chance; loaded and pointed his gun at a gull within shot; then, after a pause, he quietly laid it down, with the remark, "No, no! let the poor thing live!" One of the foremen at Hope Park furnishes an incident of later years. Walking down Preston Street, on his way to the office, Mr. Nelson saw a poor little sparrow, just fledged; and having with some difficulty caught it, he gave a boy sixpence to take it to Salisbury Green, and set it free among the trees. Another incident I glean from one of Mrs. Nelson's letters. "One day, when we were walking together in the grounds, he stooped down and lifted up so tenderly a worm which was on the gravel walk, and laying it on the lawn, he said, 'I cannot bear to see worms trampled upon; but this one will be safe here.'" This is a specific instance of what was a characteristic trait. In some manuscript "Recollections of the late William

Nelson," noted down by Mr. Dalgleish, the superintendent of the literary department of the publishing work for many years, the same familiar trait is thus referred to :—" The birds were his constant and most familiar friends. In the veranda of his beautiful house at Salisbury Green he had quaintly-fashioned rustic boxes hung up for the birds to build their nests in. It is a simple matter of fact that, not once or twice, but many times, when walking round his garden after a shower, he lifted a worm from the path, and laid it daintily on the grass." The tenderness that spared the gull, and cared for the worm on his garden path, went even beyond this. He could not bear to see a mouse-trap set, and nothing pleased him more than when his children gave evidence of a like sympathy. "None of us," writes Mrs. Nelson, "will ever forget the delight he was in one morning when he learned from Alice that she, unknown to any one, had been cutting the string with which the spring of a trap set in the nursery was held, so that no mice might be caught. The servant, on her morning visits to the room, was mortified at the failure of her plans to entrap the intruders, and only after a good deal of questioning found out the delinquent." Yet such are the curious inconsistencies of human nature, no such thoughts seem to have intruded to mar the enjoyment of his favourite pastime of fishing.

He was *en rapport* with living nature in that peculiar way that seems to distinguish an exceptional class of men. Dogs manifested for him an instinctive sympathy, and he was perfectly fearless with regard to them. When travelling with me in the Muskoka Lake district in Canada, a backwood farmer shouted a warning as he approached the kennel of a half-breed wolf-dog, such as are common with the Indians. But the animal, though ordinarily fierce, responded to his caresses. His own favourite dog, Leo, a fine Italian greyhound, watched for him, and contended with the children for a share of his attention. He would coax and whimper to be allowed to accompany him to the counting-room, where his favourite corner was behind his master in his chair at the writing table, to the manifest inconvenience and satisfaction of both. In a retired nook in the grounds the visitor would come unexpectedly upon the mound, with its little marble pillar, that marked the grave of canine favourites of earlier years, and especially of poor Bronté, whose memory was a source of bitter self-reproach to his master. William Nelson was in the habit for many years of going down to the neighbouring sea-coast before breakfast to bathe. This he did summer and winter, leaving early in the cold dark mornings, accompanied by his faithful companion, Bronté, a large Newfoundland dog. They travelled together in the train to the Chain Pier. But when Mr.

Nelson was absent from home, Bronté missed his master, and setting off at the usual early hour, took the train and went off to the beach in search of him. The fact only became known when an account was presented from the railway company for Bronté's travelling expenses. He and his master were well known to the railway officials, and so Master Bronté, as it proved, had regularly journeyed for his morning bath in a first-class carriage! But the span of life runs within straitened limits for our canine favourites, and ere the close it had become a burden to poor Bronté. The feeling associated with his death, which had long secretly preyed on his master's mind, found utterance when, in subsequent years, old age once more rendered life a burden to another household pet. A fine large tom cat had passed from kittenhood to extreme old age, and was nursed till its condition of helplessness became so pitiable that some one suggested the administration of poison as an act of mercy. "No, no! don't give it poison!" exclaimed Mr. Nelson; "you would never forget it. I have never forgiven myself for allowing poor Bronté to be poisoned. It haunts me still. I shall never forget it as long as I live." So poor Tom was left to die a natural death two days later.

Brighter associations connect themselves with a scene in the drawing-room of Salisbury Green which transpired in recent years. On a lovely Sabbath morning, when the windows were open on to the lawn, and all were assembled for family worship, as William Nelson was reading a chapter from the Bible, a starling flew into the room. It alighted and kept hopping about his chair, till all knelt down; when, instead of being startled, it perched on his shoulder, remaining quietly there all the time of prayer. When the family rose from their knees, it was thought that the bird would fly away; but it refused to quit its novel perch. He walked with it on his shoulder up to the nursery, where a large bowl of water was placed upon the table, when "Charlie," as their pet starling was subsequently named, hopped down to enjoy the luxury of a bath. A cage was procured; but Mr. Nelson would not hear of its being shut in. Ultimately, Charlie was housed in a large open cage in the laundry, with free access to the garden. There he made himself entirely at home, and became a great favourite; but after some time he flew off into the garden and did not return. One evening, at a later date, when the family were seated on the lawn, a starling—possibly Charlie—perched on one of the children's shoulders; and that was the last they ever saw of their little visitor.

There was a rare naturalness and simplicity in William Nelson. He was at ease in any company, and equally accessible to poor as to rich. Yet, with all this, he was singularly undemonstrative. As one of his old friends writes, "he was no hand-shaker;" so that a stranger could never have guessed the deep sympathies that lay concealed under his quiet manner. Yet when his pity was excited his emotion was extreme, and he betrayed the tender sensitiveness of a woman, his tears flowing unrestrained. When his mother, to whom he was passionately attached, lay dying, he shrank from entering the room, where the sight of her suffering overpowered him. But he lingered about the door of the apartment, and could not stay away. When moved with apprehension of the safety of those most dear to him—as on one occasion which I recall, when in deep anxiety about the safety of his son—his emotion was even painful to witness. But his capacity for enjoyment was equally great, and retained in it to the last much of the freshness of childhood. A "Punch and Judy," especially with a group of children enjoying the show, never lost its charm for him. Another kindly trait of unsophisticated naturalness was the pleasure he derived from street music. He would wait to listen to a ballad-singer, and after a liberal gift, ask to have the song over again. A blind bagpiper was irresistible, though more, I suspect, as an object of charity than for the charm of his music. A cornopean player and sundry German bands came regularly to his office window, and "the Rhine Watch" was sure to call forth half-a-crown. After his death, the comment of an old Parkside workman on the changes that his absence had created was summed up with the remark, " The beggars on the Dalkeith Road and the bands of music have ceased to come now."

The pleasure which he derived from music was intense. It was, indeed, no uncommon thing to see him moved to tears under its influence. But much of this, doubtless, was the pleasure of association : as in the plaintive national airs of Scotland, the songs and ballads familiar to him from childhood, and the sacred music linked to hymns, many of which have become part of the national psalmody, and entered into the religious life of the whole English-speaking race.

In art his taste was pure. He delighted to have artists about him, criticised their works with frank sincerity, and at times with an unconventional bluntness that was a little startling. Sir George Harvey, James Drummond, Sir Noel Paton and his brother Waller, Sir Daniel Macnee, Keeley Halswell, Alfred H. Forrester (Alfred Crowquill), with Doré, Giacomelli, and other foreigners, were all among his artist-friends ; and to those must be added Mrs. D. O. Hill, William Brodie, Stevenson, and other sculptors, to whom the charms of his tasteful home and its beautiful surroundings were familiar. His remarkably fine and expressive head was a model they prized to work from. His feelings in regard to artists and their works find expression in his letters from time to time, as he notes his sense of the loss created by their death.

William Brodie, a self-taught artist of great simplicity and true genius, whose fine statue of Lord Cockburn holds its place in the old Parliament Hall of Edinburgh alongside of Roubiliac's Forbes of Culloden, Chantrey's Lord Melville, and Steel's Lord Jeffrey, was engaged in 1881 on a marble bust of William Nelson. He had been commissioned to execute for Toronto a bronze statue of Mr. Nelson's brother-in-law, the Hon. George Brown, leader of the Liberal party in Upper Canada in its protracted struggle for constitutional government. His death, after long suffering, by the pistol-shot of an assassin, created a wide-spread sympathy in Canada, and awakened in the mind of William Nelson the keenest sympathy on behalf of his widowed sister. This, accordingly, gave an exceptional interest to the proposed statue. He discussed the plans with the sculptor, and eagerly anticipated its execution. But the commission had not been long intrusted to him, and the plans for its realization settled, when death arrested the gifted sculptor in the midst of his work. More than one day had been spent in the studio, examining some of his latest productions, including the unfinished bust, and discussing the treatment of the proposed statue. In the following November, William

Nelson thus writes:—" You will have heard, ere this reaches you, intelligence of the death of poor William Brodie, the sculptor. He had been suffering for several months past from fatty degeneration of the heart, and on Sunday morning last he was released from earthly care and trouble. I had a note from his wife about a week before his death, in which she stated that he was a little better, and that he had been able to make some drawings for the statue of George Brown, but that no further progress had been made in the matter. The loss is great to art, for he was at his very best, and improving as he progressed. His Sir James Simpson I do not like; but he blamed its low site, buried among the trees, and wanted it removed to the open area of Nicolson Square, where, I daresay, it would show much better. As for his Lord Cockburn, it is the finest thing in the Parliament House. It is not for me to suggest who should now be intrusted with the work; but there can be no doubt that Mrs. D. O. Hill will be looking out for the commission; and if it should come her way, and she were to produce a work equal to her statue of Livingstone, the committee would not have occasion to regret having intrusted her with it."

Art had ever a charm for William Nelson, and he watched with jealous sensitiveness the memorial statues which adorn the streets and squares of his native city. But a keen personal sympathy gave intensity to his

interest in the one to be erected in honour of his own
brother-in-law. The execution of it was ultimately
intrusted to Mr. C. Bell Birch, A.R.A.; and in February
1884 Mr. Nelson thus writes from London to Mr.
James Campbell:—" I am here for a short time, with
Mrs. Nelson and my daughter Florence. We have all
been out this afternoon at the studio of Mr. Birch, the
sculptor, seeing the model of the statue that is to be
erected to the memory of poor George Brown. I am
glad to say that we are all of opinion that the statue
will be a noble one, though we are not quite sure if the
likeness will be what can be called a speaking likeness."
The statue did ultimately satisfy in this respect, and
now forms an attractive feature in the Queen's Park
at Toronto. As to the love of art here referred to, it
is perpetuated by the younger generation. Salisbury
Green has its own studio, where both modelling and
painting were pursued by a group of young artists
with more than ordinary amateur skill. But art has
found other rivals in the new home to which the fair
critic of Mr. Birch's model has transferred her *penates.*

As time wore on, and the thick clustering black locks
of early years whitened with the frosts of time, William Nelson courted more than ever his own family
reunions, delighted to gather his friends about him,
and noted with tender regrets the blanks that death
made in the old circle. Thus he writes to me in Jan-

uary 1882: "Several weel kent faces have fled wi' the year that's awa', including old artist-friends who have recently disappeared from our midst that you will mourn." After referring to William Brodie and Sir Daniel Macnee, he proceeds: "And now I have to inform you that your old friend William Miller [the eminent engraver] has been called away, he having died at Sheffield yesterday. I met him not long ago in the Meadows, as he was going in the direction of Millerfield; and he walked as erect as he ever did, which was a most remarkable thing for a man only four years short of being a nonagenarian. In addition to those I have mentioned as having joined the majority, the name of Sheriff Hallard has to be added; and Edinburgh has lost in him a great deal of happy sunshine."

CHAPTER IX.

GLIMPSES OF TRAVEL.

REFERENCE has already been made to William Nelson's love of travel. It was indeed a passion with him, which, with his persistent eagerness for the minutest information on all points brought under his notice, might under other circumstances have won a place for him among distinguished travellers.

During a delightful sojourn which I shared with him in the Vale of Yarrow in 1880, a special object of pilgrimage was the ruined cottage in which the African traveller, Mungo Park, was born; and as he looked on it he recalled the picture, by Sir George Harvey, representing the fainting traveller in the African desert revived by the sight of a little flower that seemed to tell of the divine hand, and renewed his faith in the fatherhood of God. He followed up the subject, recovered an original sketch map executed by the traveller of his intended second route, of which he had a copy made; and among the letters preserved by him is one from Dr. Anderson of Selkirk, in which it is stated :—

"Park served his apprenticeship for a surgeon with my grandfather in this house (Dove Cot) where I now live, and where my grandfather, my father, and myself have practised for more than a hundred years. My father served his apprenticeship with Park in Peebles, when he practised there before going off on his second journey. There stands a very handsome tree in front of my house, a horse-chestnut, which was planted by the traveller while courting his intended wife."

African travel had a peculiar fascination for William Nelson. The return of the venerable missionary, Dr. Robert Moffat, from his life-long labours among the Hottentots and Bechuanas, awakened in him the liveliest interest; and his son-in-law, Livingstone, was an object of special veneration. When the startling news of Stanley's meeting with him at Ujiji was reported, it greatly excited and gratified him. And when Mr. Henry M. Stanley visited Edinburgh on his return from Africa, he received a hearty welcome at Salisbury Green. Keith Johnston, another of the explorers of the Dark Continent, who fell a victim to the deadly climate, was the son of an old friend. He watched with interest the news of his early efforts, and tenderly mourned his fate. The same summer in which the ruined cottage in the Vale of Yarrow was the object of William Nelson's curious interest, he had as his guest at Salisbury Green Mr. Joseph Thomson, then recently returned from his exploratory wanderings in previously unvisited regions to the south of the Victoria Nyanza, and gratified his intelligent curiosity, plying him with questions about the strange land and its people.

His own wanderings extended beyond the ordinary routes of the tourist. He visited Norway and Sweden on more than one occasion; travelled in Denmark and Russia, through Spain, Morocco, and Algiers; journeyed, as we have seen, in Palestine; explored Egypt and the Nile; crossed the American continent to the Pacific; and was on the eve of an extended visit to Greece and Asia Minor when his active life came to a close. His correspondence is voluminous, and supplies ample details of his experience on successive journeys; but a few illustrations will suffice for needful glimpses of personal characteristics. His journey across the American continent in 1870 has already been referred to. The Yosemite Valley, and the wonders of the Yellowstone Region, are now familiar to tourists; but at that date they were recently discovered and little known. He landed at New York on the 18th of May, had the excitement of a threatened Indian raid as they traversed the territory of the Sioux, but reached the Rocky Mountains in safety. He passed through the defiles of the mountains with unexpected ease; and then he notes: " If the passage of the Rocky Mountains has been easy, this has been made up by the crossing of the Sierra Nevada in California, which is the most difficult task in railway engineering that has yet been undertaken. These mountains are between eight and nine thousand feet high, and over these the railway passes, the roadway being in many places cut out of solid rock, with perpendicular walls of many hundred feet deep, falling straight down from the very edge of the railway." The famous Yosemite Valley he describes as "a valley of about twelve miles in length by two in breadth, that has apparently been formed by the ground sinking down to a depth of some three or four thousand feet, and leaving perpendicular cliffs all round. In these are many fine waterfalls, the largest being no less than two thousand six hundred feet high;" and after a minute description of its features, he pronounces the valley to be "one of the greatest wonders of the world." The Indians were a subject of unfailing interest. He longed to see the aborigines in their genuine condition of savage simplicity; and at a later date, when referring to this subject in a letter to Captain James Chester of the 3rd U.S. Artillery, he says:—"I send you a cutting from the *Times.* We all know that the Scotch are a practical people; but I never before, in all my reading, met with an instance of their getting the credit for goaheadness in the way referred to. The Marquis of Lorne, while Governor-General of Canada, was on the look-out for the genuine native;

and some of his first experiences, as he travelled beyond the frontiers of civilization, are thus described by a correspondent who accompanied him:—'We begin to-morrow with an address from some Indians at Little Current, on Manitoulin Island, who ought to be real, full-blooded Indians, if any faith can be put in Indian names. But probably little faith can be put in them. The mixture of races has been carried on,—more especially by the Scotch, always foremost in everything,—with so much energy that it is never easy to know whether an Indian is full-blooded, or, as some stranger to the laws of orthography and pronunciation tersely phrased it, "half Ingin, half Ingineer." In one of his speeches Lord Lorne told us of his once expressing a wish to see a real, full-blooded Indian, his first; and being rather astonished when the Canadian who undertook to gratify his wish summoned the required real specimen of the aboriginal race by shouting, "Come here, MacDonald."'"

The Falls of Niagara had no such fresh wonder as belonged to the newly-discovered marvels of California; but familiarity does not lessen their effect, and the impression produced on Mr. Nelson's mind is worth reproducing in his own words. He travelled in company with Mrs. Nelson, and he thus writes:—"One misses the true height of the falls at first—one hundred and sixty-three feet—owing to looking down upon them as they plunge into a deep gorge, in addition to their great extent in breadth. But still the impression is overpowering. Before dinner we went on to Goat Island, which divides the Horse Shoe, or Canadian Fall, from the American Fall; got over to the Three Sisters—three lovely wooded islands anchored amid the roar of waters—and then looked up the great rapids from the head of Goat Island. This I really think almost finer than the actual falls. There is no hill or rising ground visible. The flat shore scarcely seems to reach above the water's brink; and here is a great tumbling flood that looks as if it came right out of the sky, and was going to sweep everything before it. After dinner we crossed the ferry, right under the falls, and formed a more definite idea of their height. We then found our way to a spot on the Canadian side above the falls, where we looked down on the Horse Shoe Fall. It has eaten its way back into the rock; and an old residenter on the spot told us it has greatly changed since he remembered it. It now looks as though the whole mighty flood were poured into a narrow cleft, and disappears in a rising cloud of vapour, in which, when the sun is shining, there is a constant rainbow."

At Toronto attractions of a different, but not less acceptable, kind awaited him. He started for the backwoods, and fished in Lake Muskoka with his old school-mate for his guide. And on his return to

Toronto, a party of the fellow-students of early years met at dinner under his present biographer's roof. Sir Andrew Ramsay, the head of the Geographical Survey of Great Britain, chanced to be on a visit to Canada; Alexander Sprunt had come on from North Carolina to place his son at the University of Toronto; the Hon. George Brown, his own brother-in-law, was now a Senator of the Dominion; the Hon. David Christie was Speaker of the Senate; Professor George Paxton Young, and their host, were both members of the Faculty of the Provincial University; and thus, after an interval of more than forty years, the memories of school and college life were recalled, and old times lived over again, with many a humorous reminiscence, and some amusing gleanings from the record of school-mates. In a letter to his sister he says: " You may imagine with what delight I met so many of my old school-fellows, and how we did talk over the days of auld lang syne ! "

The Parisian capital is a place of too easy and frequent resort to admit of its being embraced within the range of notable explorations; but two of his visits to Paris were made under such exceptional circumstances as to claim special notice here. The first of those was his characteristic visit at the period of Prince Louis Napoleon's famous *coup d'état*. An old friend, Mr. Matthew Tait, thus briefly narrates the event:—" We all know how fond he was of foreign travel, and how he liked to watch the movements of crowds and to witness any public display. My brother accompanied him to Paris in 1851. It was at the time of the *coup d'état.* Mingling one day with the crowds that filled the Place de la Concorde, they suddenly found themselves exposed to a charge of cavalry. The crowd instantly gave way amid shrieks and yells; some of them were mortally wounded. My brother remarked to me afterwards on the coolness and self - possession of William Nelson, who seemed to have far more sympathy with the unfortunate victims than concern for his own safety."

In William Nelson's boyhood the journey to London was a formidable adventure. A youth who had achieved that feat won the respect of his companions as one who had seen the world. To have actually crossed the Channel was to be a great traveller. Rotterdam and the Hague, or Christiania and Copenhagen, by reason of the trade of the neighbouring sea-port, lay within easier reach than Paris. But steam-boats and railways have wrought as great a revolution in ideas as in experience; and in his later years a visit to Paris was no uncommon occurrence. But the circumstances were altogether exceptional when in March 1871,—the year succeeding that of his journey across the American continent,—he proceeded thither, accompanied by Mrs.

Nelson and an American friend, Mr. George Buckham of New York. The Franco-German War was over; Paris had capitulated; and this unwonted condition of things presented attractions peculiarly calculated to tempt William Nelson to witness for himself the novel scene. Happily some interesting reminiscences of the adventure are recoverable from notes furnished by both of his fellow-travellers.

They met in London on the 16th of March, and on learning that the German army had evacuated Paris, they resolved to avail themselves of the opportunity of witnessing the devastations of war, while the city still wore the aspect due to its prolonged siege. They started accordingly the following day. On reaching the suburbs of Paris they were struck with the wretched condition of the numerous soldiers of the besieging army, still bivouacked there in dirty, tattered uniforms, little calculated to suggest the idea of proud conquerors. They put up at the Hôtel Chatham; and on their way from the railway station their attention was drawn to the excited crowds in the streets and boulevards. It was soon apparent that the terrors of the siege had been succeeded by revolutionary revolt. Many wounded and dying were being carried past on stretchers. The streets were filled with citizens and soldiers gesticulating in an angry manner, and evidently ripe for violence. The very few shops that were open looked dreary and deserted; and the inhabitants had a careworn, anxious look, as though they dreaded a renewal of the terrible experiences of the siege.

About noon the travellers set out to explore the scenes still bearing evidence of the conflict so recently ended. They reached the Champ de Mars in time to see several regiments of the National Guard arrive and pitch their tents. They were survivors of the army of General Chanzy, which had suffered so terribly; and Mr. Buckham notes of them: "All were scarcely older than mere boys. They were in a dreadfully ragged and distressed condition." Everywhere, indeed, the pride and glory of war had given place to its most forbidding aspects. At Pont de Jour the shells had made terrible havoc, almost totally destroying every house in the place. At St. Cloud it was the same. The palace which the Emperor left on the 18th of July 1870, at the head of the Grande Armée, to march to Berlin, was almost completely demolished; and a street of once beautiful mansions near it was a mere pile of ruins. This was the work of the besieged, in their efforts to dislodge the Germans, who were carousing in the magnificent halls of the imperial palace. Everywhere the travellers were struck with the evidences of the blind fury of the populace. The "N," the "E," and every symbol of the emperor, had been effaced or broken. Statues of the First Napoleon, and a beautiful statue of the Empress Josephine that adorned the avenue which bore her name, had been thrown down and flung into the river. Even the heads of the bronze eagles on the Grand Opera House had been broken off.

They sought in vain for a conveyance to hire. At every livery stable they were told that the horses had all been killed and eaten. Towards evening the excitement became intense, under the apprehension that the Red Republicans, who were evidently gaining ground, would take complete possession of Paris. The landlord of the Hôtel Chatham was greatly excited, and cautioned his guests against venturing out of doors. But an old citizen of Edinburgh, Mr. Nimmo, who was well known to Mr. Nelson, undertook to be their guide. He had himself been a leader in the political movements of the old Scottish reformers at a time when such proceedings imperilled his safety; and so, taking refuge in Paris, he had resided there for forty-nine years, and now found himself at home in the *furor* of a fresh revolution. Under his escort they traversed the deserted and gloomy thoroughfares, till they reached the Place Vendôme, where a military guard arrested their progress, and compelled them to pursue a different route. When they passed the end of the Louvre, and turned in the direction of the boulevard leading towards the Place Vendôme, they suddenly became in-

volved in a disorderly mass of soldiers; and within
half an hour after they reached their hotel, the Place
Vendôme was captured by the mob.   A little later the
Hôtel de Ville was in the hands of the Communists,
the government fled from Paris, and the revolution was
an accomplished fact.   The Grande Armée disappeared.
On the Saturday night, March 18th, there was fighting
going on in several parts of the city; and when, on the
following day, Mr. and Mrs. Nelson and their friend
visited two Protestant churches, they found them
closed, and all attempt at public worship abandoned.
They were successful at length in securing a hired
vehicle, and making their way to the Jardin des
Plantes, where they found, to their surprise, that nearly
all the animals had survived the siege.   There had been
sensational newspaper paragraphs concerning the novel
dishes which the national menagerie supplied; and
William Nelson's fancy was greatly taken with the
idea of a hippopotamus steak, a giraffe ragout, a dish of
devilled tiger, or some other equally *recherché* entertainment; but instead of the beasts being devoured, it had
been found possible to provide them with something to
eat.   Eighty-four shells had fallen within the garden
enclosures, but the damage was slight; while seven of
the poor invalids in a large hospital adjoining had been
killed in their beds.   While walking through the Jardin
des Plantes, a stranger approached Mr. Nelson, and

addressing him, told him he was a professor in the University of Dublin, had been shut up in Paris during the siege, and reduced to the direst straits. He was anxious to get away, but he had no money. Mr. Buckham, who witnessed the interview, adds: "In such cases Mr. Nelson never hesitated. I have seen many other instances of his benevolence. He relieved this gentleman at once." Mr. Buckham adds that he learned from Mr. Nimmo of many instances of suffering and distress, as the results of the siege, which had been reported by him to Mr. Nelson. He did not stop to inquire more, but helped the needy, and relieved the distressed and suffering, without any idea that his good deeds were ever known to any one but Mr. Nimmo, who had the pleasant duty of acting as his almoner.

The entire scene abounded in strange and exciting novelty. They drove to the Hôtel de Ville, and there had to abandon their conveyance. The grand square was filled with soldiers. Men and boys were tearing up the paving-stones and constructing barricades. The flag of the Red Republicans was flying on the hotel, and the soldiers were shouting, " *Vive la République!* " and fraternizing with the mob. So alarming grew the situation that the idea gained favour with many of the citizens to invite the return of the Prussians to Paris as the only escape from a reign of terror. Proclamations were issued by the Government, and counter proclama-

tions by the Red Republicans. The travellers were
warned by their landlord not to venture out; but it
was useless to visit Paris at such a time merely to be
immured in their hotel. So at noon they started for
Versailles, under the guidance of Mr. Nimmo, and paid
a visit there to M. Giacomelli, Mr. Nelson's artist friend.
He had had several Prussian officers quartered on him,
and the account he gave of the insolent brutality of
those representatives of the victorious army seems to
have been abundantly confirmed by the condition in
which they left the artist's beautiful château. Mr.
Buckham thus writes:—

" Monsieur and Madame Giacomelli are people of the
highest refinement and culture, and it was impossible to
listen to a recital of their wrongs unmoved. The walls
of their *salons* were hung with most beautiful paint-
ings, many of which had been cut from their frames.
The beautiful draperies of the windows were stained
with tobacco juice; and the rich satin coverings of their
furniture, which the officers had lounged on with spurs,
were hanging in ribbons."

The calm self-control and fearlessness in danger which
have already been noted among the characteristics of
William Nelson, were repeatedly noted by his travelling
companion under the most trying circumstances during
this sojourn in Paris. Mr. Buckham thus writes:—
" In the exciting scenes of these few days, in which

Mr. Nelson mingled freely and fearlessly, no one was so calm as he. The writer accompanied him through scenes in which we were often menaced with the insane violence of armed men, so that it was deemed the height of madness to expose ourselves to it. On one occasion, in the Marché St. Honoré, which we entered suddenly, not knowing what was going on, we found it crowded with armed men and women almost foaming with rage at our intrusion. Three words uttered by Mr. Nelson in a low tone restored me to self-control. 'Take my arm,' he said quietly, and we passed unharmed, with muskets and bayonets pointed at us. While traversing the Rue de Rivoli, for a long distance we did not see a human being, until we were suddenly confronted by a Communist doing sentinel duty. Mr. Nelson said to me in his calm tone of voice, 'Say nothing; I'll manage this fellow.' So on we went, and the sentinel brought down his musket from his shoulder. Our pace was not changed. Mr. Nelson gave the military salute; he again shouldered his musket, and we passed on."

The season was early, but a succession of days of brilliant sunshine, with the trees putting forth their fresh spring leaves and early blossoms, and the songs of the birds already building their nests, all tended to intensify the desolation of the scene and the misery of the populace. In the ruined villages around Paris they saw men, women, and children who gazed as if stupified at the wreck of their humble dwellings, while they seemed only involved in worse dangers by the withdrawal of the invaders. A revolution was at its height. The National Assembly was sitting at Versailles, while the Red Republicans held Paris ; and the army was taking sides, and divided between the rival governments. On the 21st of March, Mr. Buckham notes :— " Another splendid day, but as no cabs could be found, we trudged about on foot. The streets are filled with crowds of excited people ; some are armed, and bent on mischief. Not a vehicle is to be seen ; the whole roadway is filled with people. Orators are declaiming, and the newswomen are screaming out the last 'special,' which is eagerly seized until the stock of newspapers is exhausted. The landlords of the hotels have forbidden the departure of their guests in obedience to an order issued by the Government. The English agent of the Rothschilds called and informed us that a conflict was inevitable. The people of wealth were ordered to furnish money to the insurgents, and if they refused they were marched off to the Conciergerie between two files of soldiers. Suddenly about noon the Boulevards were filled with immense crowds of citizens shouting for peace. A great procession was formed and marched to the Hôtel de Ville and Place Vendôme to remonstrate with the Communists. This movement, proving the unpopularity of the insurrection, was visible at once on the Bourse by the rise of stocks! The order forbidding strangers to depart was revoked, the shops were reopened, and there was a reasonable prospect of an immediate suppression of the revolution."

But the troubles were not over for the courageous travellers who had thus gratified their curiosity to witness for themselves the scenes of a besieged city and a Parisian Communistic revolt. On coming down to breakfast on the Sunday morning, they were gratified to meet at the breakfast table an old friend, in company with two others who, like themselves, had come to Paris to see the results of the terrible war. They were the only other guests at the hotel. On their first visit to Versailles they had had a good view of the great fortress, Mont Valérien, and explored with much interest the surrounding rifle-pits and other means of defence; and it was now proposed that the whole party should visit the fort. But Mrs. Nelson writes:—
"On reconsidering our plans, William decided that he would prefer going to Versailles; so Mr. Buckham and I set out with him, while our friends started for Fort Valérien. We found much to interest us, and did not return to our hotel till the evening. But on arriving there the landlord met us in a state of great excitement. We had, it seemed, very narrowly escaped a

novel and trying experience. Our three friends had
been taken for spies, and as soon as they reached the
fort were made prisoners. After being detained all
day, they had been released, and were already on their
way to England. He also told us that he had orders
from head-quarters that we were to leave at once." So
ended this visit to Paris in the days of the capitulation
and the Commune, not without some very exciting
experiences, and more than one narrow escape from
imminent danger. It was characteristic of William
Nelson's fearless unconsciousness of danger that he
made Mrs. Nelson the sharer in an expedition, replete
indeed with attractions of a highly novel and exceptional kind, but beset by so many dangers that nothing
but her trusting confidence in his guardianship could
have induced her to risk the exposure which it involved. As it was, it might be styled a lucky accident
which alone prevented her sharing in the uncomfortable
romance of being made a state prisoner in Fort Valérien. But such incidents have a piquancy in the
memories of later years, when the discomforts and apprehensions they involved have passed out of memory.
Nevertheless the narrow escape from incarceration in a
state prison under the later Commune was the foremost
incident in Mrs. Nelson's thoughts whenever she recalled the experiences of that exciting time.

"It was a narrow escape," she writes, "for we were

the last people to get out of Paris. The Provisional Government took the place of the Prussian invaders; and our train was the last one allowed to leave Paris. We were repeatedly taken for spies and stopped on the street. Had we gone to Fort Valérien and been made prisoners, the suspicions that had been excited would have told against us. But William never seemed to be put out, or to be conscious of danger."

CHAPTER X.

HOLIDAYS ABROAD.

A JOURNEY through unfamiliar scenes had at all times a special fascination for William Nelson; and had circumstances favoured the devotion of his early years to exploration in strange, unknown regions, it was a work that would have proved peculiarly congenial to his tastes. He had some of the most needful characteristics of an observant traveller; and his acuteness and keen desire for the thorough investigation of whatever came under notice, would have secured results of permanent value. But as it was, his later travels, even when out of the beaten track of the tourist, were necessarily the mere holiday rambles of a man escaping from the engrossing cares of business. Yet even such rambles furnish some interesting glimpses of character.

From among William Nelson's varied experiences of foreign travel in later years I select his trip to the Baltic in 1878, the incidents of which are familiar to me as his companion on the journey. More correctly, he accompanied me, starting at a few hours' notice with that indifference to elaborate preparation so characteristic of him as a traveller. We sailed from Leith on the 4th of July by the steam-ship *Buda*, bound for Copenhagen. The North Sea gave us a rough shake; but I was seasoned for the voyage by fresh Atlantic experiences, and William Nelson was a good sailor in all weathers. He was at home among the sailors on the deck or in the forecastle, and found, as usual, some objects of practical sympathy there.

The first subject of curious investigation was the famed castle of Helsingör—Hamlet's Elsinore. But it is better seen through Shakespeare's eyes, and is much too modern and prosaic to awaken any associations with Hamlet the Dane. Our traveller, who was apt to be amusingly literal on such occasions, protested against the contemptible escarpment which it offered in lieu of

> " The dreadful summit of the cliff
> That beetles o'er his base into the sea."

But Copenhagen had much to interest him; and among the rest, the recurrence of his own name, under slight modifications, suggesting the possible descent of the Covenanting farmers of the Carse of Stirling from some rough old Baltic viking. The Thorwaldsen Galleries were explored with keen interest. Then, too, I was fortunate in an early personal acquaintance with the eminent Danish archæologist, Wörsaae, which subsequent correspondence on subjects of mutual interest had ripened into friendship. He was then chamberlain to the king. So under his guidance a charming day was passed in the Rosenborg Slot, where, in addition to the choice cabinet of coins, the famous silver drinking-horn of Oldenburg, and other ancient relics, a succession of state apartments are arranged with historical portraits, arms, jewels, and furniture of the royal Danish line. Illustrated as they were by the fascinating commentary of our guide, they charmed William Nelson beyond measure. "It was," he said, "like walking down the centuries into the present time." Another day was spent, under the same instructive guidance, inspecting the richly-stored cabinets of the Prindsens Palais, where the Runic slabs from Greenland—memorials of the Northmen's pre-Columbian discovery of America— excited the liveliest interest.

On returning to our hotel on the latter occasion, we found unusual stir and excitement. We had not been aware that the Prince Imperial of France was a guest at the hotel—come to Copenhagen, as was reported, to sue for the hand of a Danish princess; and here was his Danish majesty's carriage awaiting the prince to take him to dine at the palace at the fashionable hour of 5 P.M. William Nelson remarks in a letter of the following July:—"You would see the sad fate of the

Prince Imperial; though one cannot help asking what business he had there, fighting the poor Zulus who had done him no wrong, and bringing discredit on British officers who were there on duty, whatever we may think of such duty. It seems hard to blame them for bolting—every man for himself. But you remember the little prince as we saw him at Copenhagen; he did not seem very fit to fight Zulus or anybody else, poor fellow."

The Frue Kirke occupies a prominent place among the attractions of Copenhagen, and is now associated in my mind with a characteristic little incident. The travellers had visited the church, the decorations of which, from the chisel of Thorwaldsen, constitute the main source of its interest. On the morning of the Sunday following they attended the English service; and in the afternoon his companion announced his intention to go to the Frue Kirke, and invited William Nelson to accompany him. But he refused, protesting that they should not understand a word of the service, and pronouncing the procedure to be a desecration of the day. His fellow-traveller had accordingly to go alone. The church is in the form of a Roman basilica, built under the direction of the great Danish sculptor, with a special view to its marble adornments. The sole light is admitted from ground-glass panels in the ceiling. Above the altar, in

the chancel, stands the colossal statue of Christ, with
arms extended in loving regard.   In front of each pier,
in the nave, is a statue of an apostle : St. Paul symbol-
izing the irresistible might of the truth ; St. Peter the
custodian of the symbolic keys ; the doubting Thomas,
with look of indecision and finger on his lip ; St. John
as the impersonation of love ; and the others, each
more or less skilfully suggesting some appropriate
ideal.   As works of art they are open to criticism, for
as an artist Thorwaldsen had far more of classical than
of Christian feeling.   But the absence of all gay colouring, usually so much favoured in church decoration, and
the grand scale of the works in pure white marble, so
appropriate to a place of Christian worship, produce as
a whole an effect singularly impressive in its mode of
enlisting art as the handmaid of religion.   The Lutheran
service, with its familiar hymn tunes, was simple as
that of the Presbyterian Church ; and the sermon was
obviously eloquent, though delivered in the unknown
Danish tongue.   On the wanderer returning to the
hotel, he found his friend asleep in an easy-chair, and
ventured to hint that his time had been spent to as
good purpose ; but this idea was scouted, and William
Nelson stuck to it, that the sharing in the afternoon
service of the Frue Kirke was a profanation of the day.

His interest was specially excited by the comments
of Wörsaae, on the succession of flora in Denmark, from

the *Pinus sylvestris* of the early Stone Period to that of the *Quercus robur* which accompanies the prehistoric works of the Iron Age, and has been replaced within the historic period by the beech. So a run by rail afforded him the gratification of seeing one of the fine beech forests of Denmark. But he was still more charmed with the habitual courtesy of the Dane. The Thorwaldsen Museum has refined the Copenhageners, even to the proverbial street boy. He who was at all times noticeable for that spontaneous courtesy which knew no distinction between rich and poor, was amused to learn that the travellers were guilty of an unconscious boorishness in keeping their hats on when entering a shop, or even a railway waiting-room. At their first Swedish railway station—a half-finished structure with unglazed windows—a Danish friend drew their attention to this notice: "Behall gerna hufvudbonaden pa!" which politely invited them to keep their hats on under such exceptional circumstances. The impression which this produced was recalled by an incident of a different kind, on their proceeding from Stockholm to Christiania. Their interview with custom-house officers on the frontier reminded them that Sweden and Norway are still distinct kingdoms. The simple kindly manners of the Norwegian people charmed them no less than those of the Danes. Introductions gave them access to scenes of quiet domestic life, where they learned to

11

shake hands with the host and hostess after dinner, with the salutation: "Tak for maten"—thanks for the repast. A journey northward among the mountains and fiords afforded some amusing experiences of the kindly hospitalities of the peasant proprietors. The sheaf of oats, a Christmas gift for the birds, which surmounts the gable of every Norwegian farm-house, greatly charmed William Nelson as a thing so consonant to his love for the lower animals. The wild birds struck them as very familiar, never being molested, as they were told, even by the boys. On their return to the Norwegian capital, they had occasion in one of their rambles to appeal to a stranger for direction. Their few words of Norwegian, and his more ample English, proving inadequate for the occasion, he politely undertook to be their guide; and after a walk of nearly half a mile, he turned to William Nelson to inquire the name of the person we were in search of, and lifting his hat he said: "Please you wait till I ask where he is to find."

With such experiences of Danish and Norwegian courtesy, they had not long returned to Christiania when they learned of the expected arrival of his majesty King Oscar, to open the Storthing, or Norwegian parliament. Mingling with the crowd that awaited his arrival, they were surprised at the reception tendered to their sovereign and the crown prince by those same courteous Norwegians. It was his majesty's first appearance since he vetoed a popular measure excluding the ministers of the crown from a seat in the Storthing. There was nothing menacing or rude in his reception, but the only hat taken off on the occasion was that of the king himself.

In 1882 William Nelson visited Portugal and Spain for the second time, accompanied on this occasion by Mrs. Nelson and his two younger daughters. At Cadiz, Seville, Toledo, Cordova, and other cities at which the travellers tarried, he derived intense gratification from the magnificent mediæval remains, the splendid cathedrals with their elaborately sculptured details, but above all, from the novel beauty of Arabian art. Already, at Damascus, Grand Cairo, and other Eastern cities, he had been greatly impressed with the taste and the fine elaboration of detail in the works of the Arabian architects. His rooms at Salisbury Green were enriched with tiles from the Alhambra, and with pottery and beautiful models of other works of the Spanish Moors.

The notes of Dr. Porter of Belfast have already furnished interesting reminiscences of the interchange of experiences and observations between William Nelson and himself as travellers in the East; and they are no less available for information illustrating the impressions left on the mind of the former by his Spanish tour. Dr. Porter thus writes:—" Mr. Nelson spoke to me often, and with singular enthusiasm, of his travels in Spain, and of all the wonders of art and architecture he saw there. On one occasion, I remember well, after showing me some of the exquisite models brought from the Alhambra, and also drawings of the Great Mosque-Cathedral of Cordova, and of the Alkazar in Seville, he said : ' All these are relics of the Moors, or imitations of their work. Where did they get that marvellous style of architectural decoration ? It is unique. There is nothing like it, except in those countries where the Moors were settled. The Greeks excelled it in pure taste and grandeur of idea; the Egyptians in magnitude, as at Thebes and Ghizeh ; the Assyrians in vastness and perhaps splendour; but in beauty of ornament, in delicacy of finish, in gorgeousness of interior decoration, the Moors stand unrivalled. I often wonder how, where, and at what exact period this Moorish style of architecture was conceived; in what way all its details were elaborated. One sees it in the Great Mosque at Jerusalem, in the old Arab tombs and the private houses of Damascus, in the mosques of Cairo and Algiers, and above all in the glorious Alhambra. The Greeks had their schools of architecture and art: where were the Arabs or Moors taught ? Their peculiar style, so far as I know,' he added, 'rose rapidly, almost at a bound.

We can scarcely discover any trace of progress from rude beginnings, as in the Greek architecture. This has ever been to me a most interesting and mysterious subject.'" Mr. Nelson evidently thought and read not a little upon Moorish architecture, but, like many another student, without arriving at any satisfactory result. "How the wild tribes who came up from the desert of Arabia, and occupied in succession the great cities of Syria, Egypt, northern Africa, and lastly of Spain, attained to so much taste and splendour in architecture seems a mystery." Then he remarked: "When Arab rule ceased, architecture declined in all those places, and has never been revived." He remarked more than once: "Were not the Arabs, especially those in the great cities of the East, a literary people? Had they not a multitude of books on the various departments of science and philosophy? Was not their language capable of expressing the most profound thoughts? Did it not give evidence of high cultivation?" The impress of their intellectual influence, still manifest throughout Christian Spain, attracted his notice on all hands, and especially in its ecclesiastical architecture. The Moorish artists, he observed, had furnished the models on which, after the conquest of Granada, the architects of Christian Spain wrought. When conversing about the celebrated Cathedral of Cordova, he said: "That appears to me to be one of the most remarkable buildings in Spain, or perhaps in the world. It seems to be of purely Arab architecture: in all respects like a mosque, and adapted originally for the Moslem worship. Its internal decoration too is Arab, with the flaring stripes on the walls of red and white paint, and the imitation of red and white stones in the circular arches;" and he observed that he had seen rude painting exactly resembling it in several of the private houses and on the outside of the mosques in Damascus and Cairo. Nothing different from ordinary usage, either in building or internal decoration, escaped his keen observation; but his ignorance of the language precluded him from that familiar intercourse with the people which, when opportunity offered, he ordinarily turned to such good account.

He was not unfamiliar with the beautifully illuminated mediæval Arabic manuscripts. On one occasion, when looking over Silvestre's "Universal Paleography" with myself, he remarked on the rare beauty of the Arabian illuminations, recalling his observation of them in an example shown to him in one of the mosques at Cairo; and he noted that even now illuminated manuscripts may be seen exposed for sale in the bazaars of Damascus and Grand Cairo. Dr. Porter referred to the great interest that he manifested in the work of the modern printing-press in the latter city, and the eagerness with which he inquired about the character of the books issued from the press set up there by the native Arabs. Dr. Porter told him "that there were many on medical subjects, many on interpretations of the Koran, on Mohammedan religion and morals, and one work especially which greatly pleased the common people." — "What one is that?" he asked. — "The 'Thousand and One Nights,'" was the reply. "You can hear them in every *café* throughout the East. Men act them professionally, read and recite them; and those who frequent the *cafés* always give them small presents in money."

The lack of a colloquial knowledge of the native language was a source of inevitable difficulty and trouble to the Spanish tourists; but in spite of this Mr. Nelson's observant habits were directed to some of the local peculiarities of the native dialects, and Dr. Porter notes: — "He appeared to take a great interest in the language of that part of Spain which is to a large extent peopled by the descendants of the Moors. I told him of many of the local names which are derived from the Arabic, and gave him examples of the singular changes which have been made in them to give them a Spanish form and sound. 'That accounts,' he said, 'for the peculiar pronunciation of some of those names by the people in the south of Spain, so very different from what would appear from the spelling, and from what we in this country have been accustomed to hear.' He had noticed all this in his travels, and, as was his uniform habit, tried to get at the root of everything."

But modern Spain had also its historical associations for the English traveller. In our own youthful days the war of the Peninsula and the crowning victory of Waterloo were the prominent themes in popular thought; and so William Nelson naturally turned from the exquisite remains of Arabian art to muse on the battlefields of Talavera and Albuera. After surveying the fortifications of Badajoz, he writes to his friend Captain Chester: "I could not help asking myself, What good came of all the blood shed on those two terrible battlefields, and of all who perished in the frightful siege and assault of Badajoz? Why should British blood have flowed like water for such a country and such a people as the Spaniards?" He visited Gibraltar, and passed on to Tangier; and as he notes the width of the strait and the features of the great fortress, he considers its retention by England as no longer desirable. He thus writes to his friend Captain Chester: "I took care by the way to take a good look at that so-called *precious jewel* of the British crown, Gibraltar, wondering to myself what can be the use to us of this gigantic fox-trap. The popular idea is that it commands the straits; but these are about twenty-two miles in width, there is deep water to the opposite coast, and the gun has still to be invented that can carry to such a distance. They are just now engaged in mounting a one hundred ton gun in a little fort that has been expressly built for it; but where will ever be the enemy that will allow its ships or ironclads to be brought within range of such a monster? There are to be four guns of this calibre erected on the fox-trap." He next discusses its value as a coaling-station, and thus proceeds: "We have no fewer than seven thousand troops of one kind and another immured within the walls; and there is nothing for the common soldiers in the way of amusement. Time hangs heavy on their hands, and they hate 'Gip' with a perfect hatred......I am unpatriotic enough to say that the fortress ought to be given up, as it has never been, and never can be, I am convinced, of any use to us. It cannot be said that it does more than merely command the ground on which it stands and points that can be reached by its guns."

This was not William Nelson's first visit to Spain; he had travelled through it before alone, and remembered nothing but the pleasures of the journey. But his experiences were different now, and he thus wrote to a friend soon after his return: "I have come back from my trip a wiser if not a better man; and the wisdom I have learned is that no one with a party of ladies should attempt travelling in Spain without a courier. We did not indulge in this luxury, and as none of us could speak Spanish, and as it is a rare thing for a Spaniard to learn any language but his own, the troubles that we fell into on this account were not infrequent. Again: Spaniards as a rule have no conscience, and when they have to do with parties travelling as we were, they fleece them most unmercifully; and we were not spared by them, I assure you. I need not say that the old Moorish cities of Spain are very charming, and that the people of Spain are very interesting on account of their picturesque costumes, and their being, as it were, an intermediate race between the people of the Orient and the Occident (to use two words that are rather grand)." It was characteristic of William Nelson's transparent guilelessness that it never occurred to him to make any secret of his own blunders, or to conceal the mishaps which they involved. He gave a most humorous account of the travellers' perplexities—the luggage persistently going one way and its owners another, till the ladies' troubles culminated at Madrid, where the attractions of a court reception and introduction to the state mysteries of the Palacio Real were balked by the lack of all but their travelling costume.

A later tour, in 1886, took the traveller once more to Norway, on his way to St. Petersburg and Moscow, in company with Mrs. Nelson, Florence, and their

expected son-in-law, Mr. S. F. MacLeod. On that
occasion the ancient capital of Norway, beautifully
situated on a bay in the Trondhjem Fiord, afforded him
a special object of interest in its curious old cathedral,
the most remarkable ecclesiastical edifice in Norway.
It dates from 1033, and still retains singularly interesting remains of the Romanesque work of the Northmen of the eleventh century. But it is overlaid with
many unsightly additions of a later date, well calculated to excite the critical comments of one whose
indefatigable labours were so successfully directed to
the removal of such incongruous defacements from the
ancient buildings in his own native city. Numerous
letters are available for the details of this later tour;
but there is not room in a brief memoir such as is
now aimed at for more than a few characteristic gleanings from the traveller's tale. Some of his notes on the
architecture of St. Petersburg will come under notice
in a later chapter; but one literary comment must
not be omitted here. Writing to his friend, Captain
MacEnery, he says: "The censorship of the press in
St. Petersburg is something terrible. All newspapers
and periodicals in all languages are subjected to its
tender mercies. As an instance of this, a copy of the
Scotsman posted to St. Petersburg came to us with
about three-fourths of a column blotted out, on account of some statements that displeased the great

authority as to what should or should not be read by the subjects of the emperor. A copy of *Punch* also reached us with a paragraph blotted out. It would make a grand subject for a cartoon: the emperor of all the Russias surrounded by countless thousands of armed men, and yet afraid of poor *Punch !*"

CHAPTER XI.

PARKSIDE.

ON the evening of Tuesday, the 10th of April 1878, as at the close of many a previous day, the hundreds of industrious workers in the Hope Park establishment welcomed the return of the hour of rest. The whirr of the busy machinery was stilled, and the buildings were left untenanted till the toilers with brain and hand should resume the work of a new day. The site to which the works had been transferred from the Castle Hill thirty-five years before was now crowded to its utmost limits with the warehouses, engine and work rooms of the prosperous firm. Everything seemed to give assurance of continuous success. Yet the workers were then leaving for the last time. Within a few hours the building was a pile of smoking ruins. The circumstances of this calamitous event were thus concisely narrated by William Nelson in response to a letter of sympathy: "In reference to the destruction of our printing and publishing works at Hope Park, never did fire do its work more speedily or

more thoroughly. It broke out about three o'clock
on the morning of Wednesday, the 10th inst., and in
little more than an hour the whole building was in
flames. I was aroused about a quarter past four, and
I hurried as fast as I could to the scene; but I found
when I arrived that the roof all round had fallen in,
and that flames were bursting forth from all the windows in the very front of the building. The fire broke
out somewhere in the back part of it; there was a
strong east wind blowing at the time, and this fanned
the flames and made them rush along the various flats
as they successively caught fire with extraordinary
rapidity. Not a book or sheet of printed paper was
saved!"

The calamity seemed to be overwhelming. The
splendid results of intelligent industry and rare aptitude for business had vanished, like the gourd of Jonah,
in a night. The insurance on the buildings was trifling
compared with the amount of property destroyed. But
his brother's comment on being shown the above letter
reveals a characteristic trait of William's sympathetic
and unselfish nature. "Willie's letter about the fire
recalls very distinctly that terrible morning. Poor
fellow! it was most touching to see him come up to
me before all the people and hold out his hand and
say, 'O Tom, I am so sorry for you.' He did not speak
or seem to think of himself at all."

An onlooker has preserved this little, appreciative incident : "A few of the girls who worked in the establishment were noticed standing together and weeping bitterly, when one of them, looking up, was overheard to say, as she saw Mr. William Nelson surveying the conflagration, ' Eh, there's our dear maister. I'm thinking he'll be thinking mair o' us the day than o' himsel'.' " The remark was abundantly justified ; for a friend who was near him noted that his first thoughts were of sympathy for the work-people who would be thrown out of employment ; and the feeling found practical form in his exertions on their behalf. This was characteristic of the spirit that animated him in all his relations with his work-people, and which helped to make of him an example of the very highest type of the true captains of industry. "The liberal deviseth liberal things, and by liberal things shall he stand."

The Rev. Dr. Alison, the clergyman of Newington parish, in which the Hope Park works were situated, remarked, when paying a just tribute to his memory : " I have often had occasion to remark, in visiting employés of the firm pastorally, as well as in my intercourse with heads of departments, how beautifully the idea of the Christian employer seemed to have been realized in him. The affectionate terms in which he was always spoken of were obviously the natural

return for the fairness, consideration, and generosity
for which he had become known. Being more than
a payer of wages, he got more than hirelings' service.
He was a member of another outward communion; but
there is a unity of spiritual life that ignores outward
separations. There is a Church which includes the
faithful of all churches." To one so unselfish, it was
almost inevitable that he should realize keenly the
sufferings which his own great loss must inflict on
others; and this very sympathy was his own best
protection against the blow. Nevertheless, the equanimity displayed under such trying circumstances was
peculiarly notable in one whose emotional sensibilities
were intense. The same calm composure was characteristic of him under any imposition or personal wrong,
if practised on him by a stranger. It was indeed a
common saying that nothing could anger him. One
who knew him well writes: "He had a rare power of
keeping his temper. I never saw him angry. I never
heard him utter a harsh word, except to reprobate
some mean or unworthy action. The only hard words
I can recall were in denouncing the conduct of one
whom he had regarded as a friend, and who had grossly
abused his misplaced confidence." But his equanimity
gave way when during the conflagration, in which it
seemed as if the work of a life-time was being destroyed, some one asked him if he did not suspect it to

be the work of an incendiary. The passionate emotion with which he resented the suggestion showed how keenly he was moved by the possibility that any one could be found capable of entertaining the thought of such a dastardly purpose.

The loss which the fire involved amounted to little short of £100,000; but Mr. Nelson, in describing the event in a letter to a friend, added: " I am happy, however, to state that our stereotype plates and our wood-cuts and electrotypes are all to the fore, they having been in two strong stone-built safes alongside a part of the back wall of the building, and though covered with masses of burning timber, etc., they escaped quite uninjured. With all this valuable property intact, and it forming the back-bone of our business, we will ere long be able to rear our heads again as publishers; there being no difficulty in getting all the printing and book-binding done that we will require in various offices in town here and in London. In the meantime the *débris* of the old building is being cleared away rapidly, and a new Hope Park will by-and-by appear on the site of the old one."

The new Hope Park did not, however, rise from the ashes of the old. The energy of its originators was indeed unabated. While William Nelson was contemplating, amid its smoking ruins, the suffering to be entailed on their hundreds of work-people, his brother

was telegraphing to London, Paris, and other centres
of industry, ordering fresh printing-presses and all
other newest machinery to replace what had perished.
By the favour of the city authorities temporary buildings were erected on the neighbouring Meadows. As
the new machinery arrived it was set up under what
was designed for mere temporary shelter at Parkside,
on the outskirts of St. Leonard's Hill. But speedily
the superior advantages of the new site, and the
arrangement of the works over an extended area,
instead of occupying successive floors of a quadrangle,
became so manifest that the Parkside Works were completed, with an effective architectural façade in the favourite Scottish style of the sixteenth century. Hope
Park was accordingly finally abandoned; but a graceful
memorial of the old works remains. When bidding
good-bye to the site, two beautiful pillars—the one
surmounted by the lion and the other by the unicorn
—were erected at the cost of the two brothers, at the
eastern entrance to the Meadows, as their acknowledg-
ment to the city of the timely favour extended to them
in their hour of need.

It was while the prosperous career of the great
publishing firm was arrested by this disastrous event
that a more dire calamity extended its effects far and
wide. A leading Edinburgh publisher, writing to me
shortly after the death of William Nelson, remarked:

"I need not say to you what a true, large-heârted man he was. Do you remember when their printing-house was totally destroyed, and one would have thought his own immense losses would have frozen his sympathy for other sufferers? Yet he was one of the earliest subscribers of £1,000 to the victims of the Glasgow Bank; and so far did his kindly nature long to help them, he even refused at first to discountenance the project of a state lottery on their behalf!" Their sufferings had been brought home to him in the most moving form. A letter found among his papers after his death, endorsed in touching simplicity, "Poor fellow!" is the plea of an old schoolmate for failing to appear at a High School anniversary dinner. "I have to ask you to accept my apology," he writes, "which you will readily do when I mention that I am one of the unfortunate victims of the City of Glasgow Bank; and *to-day* I have received the liquidator's final call for payment on the 22nd inst., which, I fear, will be total ruin to me."

William Nelson's local associations were strong; they attached him with passionate love to his native city. Its very stones were dear to him. Every nook and corner of it associated with his own early years, with school and schoolmates, or with the later incidents of his business career, retained a hold on his sympathies. "I send you a photograph of Edinburgh from the

Castle," he writes to an old friend beyond the Atlantic, "that it may keep you in mind of the dear old city." Hence the abrupt close of the Hope Park epoch, and the transfer to the new quarters at Parkside, awoke feelings wholly apart from those which the pecuniary loss involved. The sense of strangeness in the new locality is noticeable in more than one of his private memoranda, as in the following record of time and place: "This is the first memorandum I have written in the new room in Parkside. I came to it at a quarter to eleven o'clock on Friday, July 16, 1880. Dr. and Mrs. Wilson are at present staying with us." Curiously, it is not till upwards of two years later that the memorandum occurs of the kindling of the Parkside hearth, thus: "Fire lighted in grate in my room here for the first time, November 13, 1882."

There Mr. Nelson had to be visited to see how promptly and skilfully he administered the affairs of the great printing and publishing business which he had developed into such proportions; and, happily, notes furnished by an authoress, who did considerable literary work for the firm in those later years, enable us to catch a glimpse of him in business hours. "My first visit to his office," she writes, "was, I think, in the spring of 1883. Several persons were in attendance, waiting for orders or interviews. Owing to this circumstance, and my having formed the impression that

Mr. Nelson was a very formidable sort of a man to approach, I made my proposals in an abrupt and hurried manner. I was by no means surprised at a hasty, 'No, no; quite unnecessary at present,' and made my retreat at once. But as I was passing out, he turned from another to whom he had given some instructions in an equally concise fashion, and rising suddenly from his chair with some apologetic words, he inquired what I had published, and then said, 'I have been wishing to see you.' After this we had a long, pleasant chat, and he at once explained to me certain literary work that he wished me to undertake. This was my introduction to him. I went to him a stranger, but though my acquaintance with him was only of some four years' duration, and was mostly a business acquaintance, I soon learned to regard him as a friend. The kindness and encouragement he gave helped me greatly, because it was not the mere kindness of a 'big' publisher to a 'little' author. He was always business-like in insisting that the work done should be just as he liked it. There could be no 'scamping' work under his keen eyes. But he took infinite trouble in procuring books of reference and helping my work, and was most generous in all his dealings. On one occasion, after having undertaken some work, and having given him much trouble regarding books of reference, I found the task beyond me, and had to tell him so. I expected a scolding, and instead received a cheque ' in payment for what you have done of the book.' What I had done was merely to indicate the lines upon which the book might run. A fortnight before his death he sent me a copy of the book I ' was to have written,' with a very kind note, which I value much. The publisher's office is a terrible place to a not-confident lady-writer. Sometimes I have had to wait while Mr. Nelson was ' interviewing,' directing, correcting, and so forth ; and my courage has not been strengthened by the spectacle of faulty work being overhauled in a most careful manner, and ruthlessly condemned or sharply criticised. Yet I have always gone out of that office with a light heart. Some kindly word about my children or my old home, some chat about the foreign lands he had visited, the gift of a book, a fatherly caution ' not to work too much '—these made me feel that Mr. Nelson took his large heart into the publisher's office. Would that all publishers did like him."

But the critical sharpness, and the abrupt manner of the man of business, preoccupied with the responsibilities of so large an establishment with endless claims on its directing head, all disappeared so soon as he had satisfied himself that his instructions were being rightly carried out. The new Parkside Works were within

easy distance of Salisbury Green; and the claimants on
his ever-ready charity speedily learned to know the
time when he could be waylaid in his walk to or
from the counting-room, and beguiled with a piteous
tale. Mr. Gray, for many years the faithful head of
the financial department, thus writes: "To old servants
in the works he opened his purse freely. Women who
had been employed in early days at the Castle Hill
were held by him in special favour, and I have often
seen him give them a pound note, sometimes when it
was doubtful if they would make the best use of it.
The plea that they had worked at one time at Hope
Park was a frequent claim of beggars; and many is the
silver piece that has been given away to such folks.
One adept at begging came to him, her tatters soaked
and leaky slippers dripping with rain. She told a
piteous tale, and pleaded she was the widow of a ma-
chineman in the firm's employment thirty years before.
The plea was irresistible; but the voluble manner in
which the woman overacted her part aroused his suspicions after he had responded to her appeal. 'What
sort of a man was your husband?' asked he. 'Oh, a
good, a very good man!' 'Ay; was he tall or short?—
as tall as that man?' pointing to a man about six
feet high who had just entered. 'Yes!' responded the
woman, 'he was a braw, tall man.' 'Give me back the
money!' he exclaimed with unwonted severity of tone,

as he recalled the fact that the old machinist was much below the ordinary stature; and the impostor was ordered to the door."

His unstinted liberality in all philanthropic and missionary work was wholly unaffected by denominational or party limits; and hence he was liable to be preyed upon by genteel foreigners claiming to be in temporary pecuniary distress, and still more by clerical impostors. When he had reason to think he was imposed upon, he would search into the matter with the utmost keenness; though rather, as it seemed, with a desire to satisfy himself of the truth, than with any purpose of stinting his liberality in the future.

One morning, as the family sat at breakfast, a servant came into the room, and alarmed Mrs. Nelson by whispering to her that there were two detectives at the door who wished to see her. Her manner must have betrayed her apprehensions, for one of them laughed and said, "Don't be frightened, Mrs. Nelson; we have only come to ask you to use your influence with your husband, and try to get Mr. Nelson to give up giving money to respectable-looking beggars. There is a register kept by a man in the High Street of all the 'giving people' in Edinburgh. That is the first resort of this class of beggars. By paying half-a-crown, they are allowed to take a note of the names and addresses, and Mr. Nelson's stands at the head of the list!" He undertook to look more sharply after the smooth-tongued gentry in black, though, it is to be feared, with only partial success. He manifested a sensitive repugnance to wealthy people whose riches were of no use to any one but themselves; but he protested, to the amusement of his friends, that he strongly disapproved of promiscuous charity. He had his own rules of action. A maimed or deformed person, the blind, the deaf-mute, or any one incapacitated in the struggle for life, he conceived could never be wrongly helped. A poor widow, an old employé, or the widow or orphan of any of his old work-people, had an irresistible claim on his liberality; and other pleas were readily forthcoming to justify the deed of charity to his conscience. But he took pains to search out genuine objects of commiseration; and many of his charities were unknown even to members of his own family. One Saturday afternoon, when walking home with Mrs. Nelson, he asked her to wait while he went in to a humble dwelling. When interrogated as to the object of his visit, it was ascertained that he had been giving a poor widow money to pay her rent; and on further inquiry it turned out that he had been paying it regularly for years. Nor was this a solitary case, as became known when death closed the liberal hand that had so often made the widow's heart leap for joy. Charity was in him a spontaneous impulse of kindly sympathy

which, while exercised not only unobtrusively but with
a sensitive shrinking from recognition, was carried out
on too great a scale to escape observation. The difficulty of his biographer is to select from the varied
instances at his disposal. " I saw him once," writes a
lady, " as he was walking along Clerk Street, pause at
a confectioner's window, where a poor little ragged
urchin was standing gazing wistfully at the cakes in-
side. One kindly hand was laid on the boy's shoulder;
the other took a silver piece from his pocket. A few
words were spoken, and Mr. Nelson passed on, while
the boy darted into the shop; and I had the pleasure
of seeing him come out a moment later already devouring one of the cookies of which he had become the
delighted possessor." He was never known to refer to
such acts. They were, indeed, of too frequent occurrence to seem to him worthy of note. The poor and
needy had learned to regard him as their unfailing
resort; and if his charity was abused, he would say in
reply to prudent remonstrants that it was better a few
impostors should succeed, than one genuine claim be
rejected.

The traders on his benevolence were wont, as already
noted, to watch for him on his way to Parkside; and
Mr. Gray notes of such claimants: " Mr. Nelson would
sometimes say to me, ' The printing trade must be in
a dreadful state,' for in his walk thither he had been

met by half-a-dozen printers pleading for help. He inquired at times into the state of the trade, with the view, I suppose, to guide him in his charities; for it offended his guileless trustfulness in others to find he had been imposed upon, though it never led to any stint in his liberality." Another who had been many years in his service writes: "He had an almost child-like confidence in some folks; but if his suspicions were once aroused as to anything wrong, he ferreted out the matter to the bottom, and in case of any betrayal of trust, he would speak of it with a keen sense of wrong. But if you responded with any denunciation of the offender, his manner changed, and he generally found some apology or some reason for pitying the delinquent. Nor did the fact that a claimant had wronged him affect his consideration of the case if it proved to be a necessitous one, especially if he had a wife and children." When an action was raised by the contracting engineer who undertook the repairs of the machinery, against the widow of his predecessor, to enforce the completion of some work for which her late husband had been responsible, William Nelson opposed it, declaring that no good ever came of prosecuting a widow, and he ultimately repaid £130 of law expenses incurred in the suit.

Under the system which such a spirit naturally developed, the relation between master and servants

assumed a very different aspect from that of the mere
hireling. The workers in his employment cordially
sympathized in his success, and took a pride in contributing to the prosperity of the firm. A gentleman,
whose intimate relations with it for many years made
him familiar with its internal economy, thus writes:
" The claims of his own work-people at Hope Park or
Parkside were never disregarded. He had, as the firm
still has, a host of pensioners: aged employés, and the
widows and children of former workmen, who were
mainly dependent on his charity for their daily bread.
Groups of them, or of their representatives, still assemble in the entrance hall at Parkside on the pay-day,
by whom his name is revered. They tell their own
tale of satisfaction and gratitude." The charity which
thus began at home did not end there. The difficulty,
indeed, is to select from the examples communicated
to me. One characteristic instance I owe to a fellow-
traveller, who found himself in company with William
Nelson in an Italian town during a festive season.
It was a scene of holiday rejoicings; but it did not
escape Mr. Nelson's notice that while the mass of the
people were enjoying themselves, there were a number
of uncared-for poor whose misery was made the more
apparent by the festive scenes that surrounded them.
This so impressed him that he forthwith made arrangements with a hosteller for the entertainment of the

ragged lazaroni. Another gentleman who passed some weeks with him at one of the German spas tells this story:—" At the little English church there was a clergyman stationed, entirely dependent on the free-will offerings of the ever-changing congregation. There were no resident members to act as churchwardens or vestrymen; so, after the service, the poor clergyman himself went round and collected the offertory. This was too much for Mr. Nelson. He volunteered his services, which were accepted. To the clergyman's agreeable surprise, the collection increased amazingly; and he only learned where the increase came from by a return to the old scale after Mr. Nelson's departure."

It was a curious study to note the guilelessness and child-like simplicity which William Nelson retained unchanged to the close of his life, along with rare shrewdness and sagacity as a man of business. Whenever any transaction assumed a business aspect, however trifling might be the amount involved, he was prompt, clear-sighted, and acute, detecting and with quiet firmness resisting any attempt at overreaching or fraud. On one occasion, when I was his fellow-traveller, a knavish newsboy to whom he had intrusted a sixpence decamped without returning the change. This breach of faith provoked a display of indignation so entirely disproportionate to the value of the loss, as obviously suggested to our wondering fellow-travellers in the

railway carriage that they witnessed another Shylock
bemoaning his lost ducats.   They little knew that the
rogue, by the invention of a pitiful tale, might have
transmuted the stolen coppers into gold.   This transparent naturalness of character revealed itself equally
in his intercourse with high and low.   Alike at home
and abroad he was often brought into familiar relations
with men of rank and distinction, and his engaging
manners and wide culture made him a welcome addition to any company.   But there was no change in his
manner towards the nobleman or the skilled artisan.
An old friend notes of him what many will recall :—
" Reverence was part of his nature.   However intimate
he might be with a friend, he scarcely ever addressed
him, personally or by letter, except by full name as
Mr. or Dr.; and it was the same with his own employés.   The Dick or Tom of his fellows in the work-
room was Richard or Thomas, if not Mr. ——, when
spoken to by him."   His circle of friends included men
of the most dissimilar social positions; and his intercourse with some of his old workmen whose integrity
and worth had been proved by long experience was of
the most intimate and confidential nature.   No wonder
that he was faithfully served.   He practically demon-
strated his belief that,—

> " The rank is but the guinea's stamp ;
> The man's the gowd for a' that."

He entertained at his table the publishers, booksellers, and others with whom he had business relations. Mr. David Douglas thus notes his recollections of him and of his kindly hospitalities: "He was the one to whom any of us would have gone in difficulties or doubtful trade questions, feeling sure that he would not only give sound advice but kindly sympathy. Many such cases occur to me. He used to gather round his table annually the various members of the printing and publishing trades; and I used to admire his true hospitality in making every one, from the youngest guest to the oldest, as much at home as possible, gently drawing out their best stories, and exchanging with genial humour some pleasant talk with all." In his Saturday visits to the Castle of Edinburgh in connection with his restorations, referred to in a subsequent chapter, the most eminent archæologists, artists, and literary men, along with his choice personal friends, responded to his welcome invitations. At times the company included such distinguished additions as Lord Rosebery or Lord Napier and Ettrick, who took a special interest in the work. But it would never occur to him that any spirit of social caste could influence such a gathering, and his own list of friends always included some of his trusted workmen from Parkside.

A lady whose services as an authoress brought her into frequent contact with Mr. Nelson, after noting his liberality in all business transactions with herself, adds a little incident of her personal experience. His love of dogs has already been noted; but it might have been assumed that however welcome their companionship might be at Salisbury Green, the intrusion of stranger dogs into his room at Parkside in business hours could hardly fail to be resented. Her own experience, however, is thus narrated: "I had taken my dog with me one morning; a large brown spaniel, Rover by name. He is not a general favourite among my friends, being rather boisterous in his greetings, to say nothing of his muddy paws in wet weather. His place therefore was generally without, and his intrusion into Mr. Nelson's room was undesigned on my part. Contrary, however, to his usual experience, Rover obtained a most cordial reception. A messenger was sent out for biscuits for him; and I rarely afterwards received a note from Mr. Nelson asking me to call which did not end with the invitation, 'Please bring doggie when you come.' It was no wonder therefore that Rover soon learned to feel himself at home there, and never willingly passed the door when we walked in the direction of Parkside." After noting acts of kindness and liberality to herself, she thus proceeds: "My intercourse with Mr. Nelson was only that of a business acquaintance, yet I can truly say, when I saw him carried to his grave that September day, I felt that I had lost a friend. And this, I am sure, was no rare feeling among those thus brought into business relations with him. One trait often struck me—the kindly manner in which he always spoke of his large staff, as one name or another might come up in conversation. 'The right man in the right place,' he would say, or some other hearty term of appreciation; and it was evidently no taskmaster who was over them, but rather a sort of patriarch dwelling among his own people, sure of their loyalty and affection."

Testimonies of a like kind have reached me from very diverse sources, all pointing to kindly relationships between this true captain of industry and his employés, such as seem, without exaggeration, to have realized in these days of mere trading rivalry something akin to the fealty of knightly service in the olden time. The golden rule of ever doing the right was carried out with unconscious simplicity. Mr. Gray, who, as cashier at Hope Park and Parkside, was familiar during many years with all the financial details of the business, thus sums up his testimony to the habitual business life of his old master and friend: "He was eager to avoid anything that could possibly bear the aspect of sharp practice, or allow the faintest breath of suspicion of unfairness or shabby dealing; and his generous, large soul won for the place a reputation of uprightness and honour."

CHAPTER XII.

CIVIC INTERESTS.

AS a citizen William Nelson was ever ready to forward whatever appeared calculated to promote the public welfare; and his faith in the Divine maxim that righteousness exalts the nation knew no limits in its practical application. He judged his fellow-men, moreover, by his own high standard of rectitude; and, with his faith in humanity, he was prepared to favour the largest popular concessions. In politics accordingly he heartily sympathized with the Liberal party, and frankly gave expression to his opinions on all the great questions of the day. His numerous letters to his friends abound in discussions showing the keenest interest in all the events and movements that engaged public attention: the scientific discussions and religious controversies; the triumphs of engineering skill; the fascinating novelties of geographical exploration; or again, the Crimean War, the Indian Mutiny, the great American Civil War, the Franco-German War, the Eastern question in all its phases, and the no less

momentous issues of party strife at home. In a letter,
for example, of May 13th, 1886, addressed to his fellow-
traveller, Major MacEnery, in which he gives him the
latest information about their poor old dragoman,
Abdallah, he thus writes: "I earnestly hope that
there will soon be an end of the turmoil that there
is at present in regard to Old Ireland, by letting her
people have Home Rule to the fullest extent. There
can be no harm in this; and we who are north of the
Tweed will be a great deal the better too of having
the management of our own affairs a great deal more
in our own hands, as it is absurd that we should have
to apply to Parliament for its sanction for many things
that it knows little or nothing about; and a deal of
money would be saved were applications to Parliament
for them not to be necessary. The bill for the sewage
of a district, for instance, in the south part of our city
had to be got through Parliament lately; and what
can that august body know about this odoriferous
subject? We are much more familiar with it ourselves." His appeal in such questions was apt to be to
common sense; and when practical aid was needed,
his purse was ever available. His sympathy with the
working-classes found its most fitting expression in
his dealings with those in his own employment.
When the works at Hope Park were in flames, more
than one onlooker reported overhearing the remark by

some of his work-people, that they were sure he would feel it as much for their sakes as his own. A lady visiting a poor woman in the neighbourhood of the Hope Park works, whose husband was ill, was told by her: "He works for Mr. Nelson; and they dinna let their men suffer when they canna work." Another told her that the aged and the crippled or maimed were found employment at the Parkside Works, "for Mr. Nelson can aye find a job to suit a' sorts." The evils of improvidence and the misery resulting from the drinking habits that prevailed among the lower classes were constant subjects of thought. He systematically exerted himself to devise innocent pastimes, and to stimulate the working-classes to more refined tastes and intellectual sources of enjoyment. His New-Year's letters to friends always included some reference to the midnight gathering around the Tron Church in the High Street of Edinburgh for the "first-footing," with its customary excesses, at the inauguration of the New Year; and every symptom of improvement was hailed with delight. The movement accordingly for displacing the taverns by "workmen's homes" and coffee shops met with his heartiest encouragement. A Glasgow paper-maker mentioned to a friend that he had not seen Mr. Nelson for many years, when on the occasion of a visit to Edinburgh he went into one of the places then being established under the name of

" British Workmen's Houses " for the supply of non-
intoxicating refreshments. To his surprise he found
Mr. Nelson seated there in company with one of his
daughters. On his expressing some surprise, Mr.
Nelson said he had come to see how things were
served; and that really he thought the coffee very good,
and indeed, he said in his hearty way, he thought the
milk quite as good as what they got at home from
his own cows. He was not without a hope that one
of the results of his reviving the popularity of St.
Bernard's Well, hereafter referred to, would be the
promotion of the same good end. It is not therefore
to be wondered that Mr. Nelson's services were sought
for in public life, and his fellow-citizens repeatedly
manifested the high esteem they entertained for him
by urging his acceptance both of civic and parlia-
mentary honours. But few men ever shrank more
sensitively from publicity, and only when the impor-
tance of the question under discussion overpowered
his natural reserve could he be induced to take any
part in a public meeting. Such, however, was the
high sense of his services as a citizen that he was
selected by her Majesty for the honourable distinction
of Deputy-Lieutenant of the County of Edinburgh.

But his appreciation of the antique beauty and
historical associations of his native city overcame all
his retiring dread of publicity whenever they were

endangered; and the same regard for the amenities of
civic architecture, and the dread of the destruction of
whatever is associated with the memorable events of
bygone times, repeatedly find expression in his critical
notes from abroad. In 1873 he writes to Mr. Campbell from Vienna, describing a two months' Continental
tour, in which he was accompanied by Mrs. Nelson and
his daughters Eveline and Meta. He passed from Paris
and Geneva to Italy; spent some time in Florence and
Venice; travelled as far as Naples; and then returned
to Rome. "I need not say," he writes, " that Rome,
which is really the capital of the world for art and
archæological interest, detained us much longer than
any of the other places. I was there twenty-three
years ago, and though great works are now in
progress, I may say that there has been as yet no very
great change since that time. The city, however, is
now under Italian government, and in a few years
Rome will be completely altered. There are large
buildings in course of erection near the railway station,
which are understood to be the commencement of an
entire new city in that quarter; and in many of the
streets throughout the city are marks on the houses,
indicating that they are either to be wholly or partially
demolished for improvements, or for the widening of
the streets. But I must say that from what I have
seen of the new buildings recently erected in Rome the

architecture is of about as poverty-stricken a kind as can well be imagined. They are constructed of brick, which is plastered over, and the plaster gets a coating of size of a pink hue very much like that of blot-sheet; and the effect is anything but cheering. The windows have nothing round them but plain mouldings, and these are painted gray. There is not the slightest attempt at architectural ornament externally in any of the new buildings that I happened to see. If this sort of thing goes on to any great extent, the fine mediæval feeling that there is about Rome as it now exists will be in a great measure done away with, and it will present in many parts a smooth-shaven and very unattractive appearance. The main things notable in the way of change, besides the new buildings to which I have referred, since I was in Rome formerly, are the excavations in the Forum and the Palace of the Cæsars, the Baths of Caracalla, and the changes caused by the occupation of the city by the Italian troops, and the disappearance from the streets of the religious processions, which are not now permitted. We hurried on to Rome in order to be there at Easter week, expecting to see something of the religious ceremonials for which that week has been famous for ages; but though we were in Rome the greater part of it, we found it nothing more than an ordinary week, as far as religious ceremonials are concerned. The Pope

and his council are in the sulks, and as processions in
the streets are not allowed, they have taken care that
the curiosity of strangers shall not be gratified by any
great ceremonial in the churches. It would interest
you much to see the ruins of the Palace of the Cæsars,
now that they have been cleared out, especially that
part of them which is known to have been the court
house. The wall all round still exists to some extent,
as do also portions of the mosaic floor, and the place
where the emperor or the judge sat is still to be seen.
There is in front of it a portion of the marble balustrade that extended across this part of the court; and
Dr. Philip, missionary to the Jews in Rome, who acted
as guide to us in our wanderings through these
immense ruins, said there can hardly be a doubt that
Paul stood before that very balustrade and pleaded his
cause before Nero as his judge. The guard-rooms of
the soldiers of what is called the Palace of Tiberius
are quite entire, and on the walls of them are several
very interesting scratchings made by the occupants of
those rooms in ancient days. One is of a Roman
galley in full sail; another is an outline portrait said
to be of Augustus Cæsar; another is a caricature
likeness of Nero; and another a very clever comical
figure of a fellow with a tremendously long nose.
What a living reality they seem to give to those old
times! In a room at a little distance there is a

remarkably clever scratching of a donkey with a mill on its back, with the words below : 'If you labour as I do, you shall not want bread.' How little things of this kind carry us back to the far bygone past!"

In like manner, in a letter to Dr. Simpson, he thus records the impression which his visit to St. Petersburg in 1884 left on his mind : " We were very much disappointed with St. Petersburg, as it occupies a site that is very flat and very unhealthy ; and it is a city of pure sham, so far as the architecture of it is concerned. The principal buildings, as a rule, are of plaster or cement, and are painted in a style that is perfectly barbaric. Even the celebrated Winter Palace is not an exception. It is of Roman architecture ; and it is besmeared with paint of a yellowish-brown colour which is sufficient to make one shudder. The building, moreover, is of great extent, and it is all the more repulsive on this account."

But if the disfigurement of the modern city of Peter the Great on the Neva, or the effacement of the historic antiquities of Rome, offended his taste, and gave rise to unavailing regrets, every movement of a like kind affecting his native city roused him not only to vehement protest, but to vigorous action to avert as far as possible the threatened mischief. Under such stimulus, all reserve disappeared, and he stood forth as the resolute defender of his city and its historical memorials. His letters to old schoolmates, whose lot had been cast far from those favourite haunts of early years, are frequently devoted to a notice of the rescue of some threatened antique building, or a wail over the irrevocable destruction of some historic pile in the alleys or closes of Old Edinburgh.

The old Bowhead land had an interest of its own, apart from its singular picturesqueness as an example of the civic architecture of older centuries. When its demolition could no longer be averted, he rescued from the wreck some of its substantial oak timbers, and had them fashioned into antique furniture as memorial gifts to absent friends. In 1883, another of the venerable survivals of older generations, immediately adjoining the former Castle Hill establishment, was demolished; and he thus records the event in a letter to myself:—
" I sent you a *Scotsman*, with an account of the demolition of one of the old houses that you will remember on the Castle Hill. It stood in front of Milne's Court, looking down the West Bow, and presented a very picturesque front, both to the street and to the court behind. Two stone-vaulted shops faced the street, standing some feet back from the pavement. It was thought that the main walls of the house went straight up all the way, and that the timber front, projecting story by story farther into the street, was an addition of later date; but this was a mistake, for the original

beams extended right over the pavement. The like-lihood is that there was an open veranda on each flat, though it had been closed in with lath and plaster in course of time. On the second flat, when the plaster was removed, it was interesting to see a neatly-carved oaken balustrade, that had been covered up probably for centuries, where one could fancy the good folks of the house sitting in their balcony enjoying the fresh air and having their gossip on the great events of the day. They could look down the Lawnmarket and the West Bow and up the Castle Hill; and it must have been a choice place on great occasions, when a royal cavalcade came up the Bow, or when some poor rogue went down it for the last time." (In allusion to the old site of the gallows in the Grassmarket.) "I see, on turning to your 'Memorials of Edinburgh in the Olden Time,' that it belonged to a worthy old citizen, Bartholomew Somerville, a liberal benefactor to our University in its early days."

The sympathetic interest thus manifested in every ancient feature of the special haunts of his boyhood extended to whatever contributed to the picturesqueness and beauty of his native city. One who was very familiar with his indefatigable exertions for the con-servation of whatever pertained to its historical antiquities—Mr. D. Scott Moncrieff—thus writes in reply to a request for information relative to the share

borne by Mr. Nelson in recent efforts on that behalf:—
"It is no easy matter to do this, for Mr. Nelson for
many years took an active interest in every movement
having for its object the enhancement of the beauties
of his native city. As you are aware, he was long
a member, and latterly one of the council, of the
Cockburn Association, founded in 1875, for promoting
the improvement of Edinburgh and its neighbourhood;
and as convener of the council I had frequent oppor-
tunities of hearing his views upon such questions. His
interest was much engaged, in particular, in the improvement of Edinburgh Castle, the Meadows, and
other public parks, the encouragement of a higher
style of architecture, and the frustration of mean and
tasteless designs, vulgar advertisements, and the de-
praved habit of painting stone work. He strove to
obviate the necessity for unsightly workshops and tall
chimneys, for which in his own extensive works there
was found no place." But he soon discovered that
mere criticising, remonstrating, and suggesting improvements were of little avail; and as Mr. Scott
Moncrieff adds: "His interest in the work of the
Association was not confined to attending meetings
and expressing his views. Every citizen of Edinburgh
may well feel proud and grateful that amongst them
there was one gifted, not only with an exquisite taste
for all that was beautiful, but with an enthusiasm in

having his aspirations given expression to, and also with the means of carrying his ideas into effect." One of those practical demonstrations of his public-spirited liberality has a history of its own.

The circular panel of the finely-carved mantle-piece in the council room of Heriot's Hospital is filled with a painting which perpetuates the tradition that the medicinal spring of St. Bernard's Well, on the Water of Leith—resembling in character the famed Harrogate springs—was discovered by a party of Heriot boys while sporting on the bank of the stream. A more dubious legendary tale assigns the origin of the name to the occupation of a cave on the neighbouring slope by the saint still associated with its healing waters; but its medicinal virtues are noted for the first time in the *Scottish Magazine* for 1760, at which date the water seems to have been in great repute. The old Scottish judge, Lord Gardenstone, an eccentric valetudinarian, having derived much benefit from the medicinal waters, in 1789 erected over the healing fountain a fine Doric temple, designed as a reproduction of the famous Sibyl's Temple at Tivoli. A colossal plaster statue of Hygeia was placed within the columns, over the vaulted chamber of the well. Thus enshrined, it has ever since been a favourite morning resort; and William Nelson continued for many years to be one of its most faithful frequenters. But the picturesque and richly-wooded valley of the Leith, to which the Heriot boys resorted in the eighteenth century, has long been invaded by the extended new town. The temple had fallen into disrepair, and the boys of the neighbouring village of Stockbridge had defaced and mutilated the statue, till it presented some of the most familiar characteristics of a genuine antique. The amenities of the spot had suffered in all ways, and the proposed erection of a public laundry on the adjacent area threatened the final ruin of the well, when in 1885 Mr. Nelson interposed, purchased it and the grounds in its vicinity, restored and beautified the well, and commissioned Mr. Stephenson to execute a marble statue of Hygeia, to replace the mutilated goddess of earlier days. The surrounding grounds were tastefully laid out, under the directions of a skilled landscape gardener, and the whole finished at a cost of £5,000, and presented to the city. He did not live to see the fine statue placed on its pedestal; but his letters to his friends frequently refer to it, along with others of the various works of restoration which so largely occupied his thoughts and engaged his active sympathy in his later years. Writing to Captain Chester in January 1886 he says: "I send you the last report of the Cockburn Association, from which you will see that I have in hand the restoration of several ancient buildings in the Castle, and of the mineral well on the Water of Leith called St. Bernard's Well, a chromo-lithograph of which I enclose. I am glad that it has fallen to my lot to do something ere I be 'called hence to be no more,' for the beauty and interest of mine own romantic town."

The shrine of his favourite healing fountain had been restored to far more than its pristine beauty, and the generous benefactor to whom the work was due had himself been "called hence," when the convener of the Cockburn Association wrote: "What Mr. William Nelson undertook he did well and thoroughly; and so long as Edinburgh citizens look down upon the valley of the Water of Leith, his work at St. Bernard's Well will keep his memory green in their hearts."

But, as his letters show, other and still more extensive and costly restorations engaged William Nelson's practical liberality, and continued to be objects of deepest interest to him till the close of his life. So early as 1847, attention had been recalled, in the "Memorials of Edinburgh in the Olden Time," to the fact that the ancient hall of the palace in the Castle still existed, though so defaced and overlaid by later transmutations as to have passed out of knowledge of the living generation. But the matter was once more forgotten till near the close of 1883, when Lord Napier and Ettrick published in the *Scotsman* an account of his explorations above the modern ceiling of the hospital ward, where, "on creeping up a ladder, through a trap-

door, he found himself in a maze of mighty beams, on
which the dust of centuries lay thick and soft." It was
the fine old open timbered ceiling, of carved chestnut,
of the great hall of the Castle. Public attention was
now keenly awakened to the interest of this historic
relic. Here was the *aula Castri*, or great hall of the
Castle, where there is little doubt the Scottish Parliament assembled in 1437 to inaugurate the reign of
the young king, James II. Here, too, if the legend is
to be accepted as a verity, only two years later Chancellor Crichton had the fatal symbol of the bull's head
served up for the Earl of Douglas. It was here that
Charles I. held his coronation banquet in 1633, and that
Argyle entertained the Lord Protector Cromwell in
1650. Of the historic worth of the ancient hall there
could be no question; and not only its degradation to
the purposes of a garrison hospital, but the general
neglect and disfigurement of the Castle, had long been
a subject of public complaint.

The council of the Cockburn Association followed
up the letter of Lord Napier with a memorial to the
Marquis of Hartington, then Secretary of State for
War, complaining of the misappropriation and deface-
ment of the ancient hall, and urging its restoration.
But the wonted formalities and circumlocution of
official correspondence ensued, with little prospect of
any satisfactory result, "when," as Mr. Scott Moncrieff

writes, "we were still hoping that the building might be rendered available for uses more in harmony with its history and associations; and while the matter was still under the consideration of the authorities, Mr. Nelson, knowing the well-nigh insurmountable obstacles in the way of Government dealing effectively, timeously, and reasonably, in affairs of the kind, in the most generous and patriotic way offered at his sole expense to undertake the restoration, not only of the old Parliament Hall, but also of two other most interesting and picturesque features of the Castle, the Argyle Tower and St. Margaret's Chapel.

The little oratory of St. Margaret had been a subject of interest to him from the time when it was anew brought under notice, in 1845, as a long-forgotten historical relic; and as for the Argyle Tower, it was associated in his mind with the reverence due to the martyrs of the Covenant. The fine old Edinburgh cemetery, the Greyfriars' Churchyard, was only separated from the West Bow by the Grassmarket, where in the seventeenth and eighteenth centuries the public gallows was erected, for the execution not only of degraded criminals, but of many of the victims of intolerance in Covenanting times, to whom a common grave was assigned in the neighbouring cemetery. There, accordingly, in happier days the Martyrs' Monument was erected, with its tribute to the memory of "about a

14

hundred noblemen and gentlemen, ministers, and others, noble martyrs for **Jesus** Christ," all executed at Edinburgh, "from **May** 27th, 1661, that the most noble Marquis of Argyle was beheaded, to the 17th February 1688, that Mr. James Renwick suffered." It was but a step from the early home in the West Bow to the Greyfriars' Churchyard, where the Martyrs' Monument had been an object of veneration to William Nelson from his youth. The same spirit of reverent piety which led to the erection of the Martyrs' Monument on the spot selected, as a mark of ignominy, for the graves of the victims of Stuart persecution, associates the name of Argyle with the tower in the neighbouring fortress in which Archibald, Earl of Argyle, was imprisoned before his execution in 1685. He had gone up to London to pay his homage to Charles II., relying on the indemnity which had been granted, as far as England was concerned. But Scotland was still a separate kingdom; and as a prominent leader of the Scottish Covenanters, Argyle was regarded with special antipathy. He was accordingly arrested, cast into the Tower, and from thence transferred to the state prison in the Castle of Edinburgh. It was from that prison chamber that the earl addressed to his friends letters marked by a rare spirit of calm Christian resignation, including the simple farewell note to his own son, written immediately before his execution. Of the latter

William Nelson had a facsimile made. Still more, according to current belief, it was in the same prison chamber that a member of the council, on coming to interview him, was startled at finding the victim of intolerance calmly asleep immediately before he walked with quiet composure to the scaffold. The scene associated with such memorable occurrences appealed to William Nelson's religious no less than to his archæological sympathies; so that the restoration of the Argyle Tower was for him, in a very special sense, a labour of love.

The work thus generously undertaken proceeded slowly, amid endless official routine and red-tape formalities. Plans were prepared and submitted to the critical revision of his colleagues in the council of the Cockburn Association before asking official approval. But hospital accommodation had to be found elsewhere; and the patience he manifested, and the calm perseverance with which he overcame the *vis inertiæ* of the Circumlocution Office, were a source of admiration to his friends and of amusement to himself. His unostentatious liberality, along with the taste and judgment he displayed, naturally gave weight to his opinions; and, notwithstanding his instinctive reserve, he was induced on more than one occasion to remonstrate with the authorities on plans that had received official approval. In 1887 the sketch of a tasteless design for a new entrance gateway, to form the main approach to the Castle, had been exhibited without attracting public attention. The working plans had been withheld; and it was about to be proceeded with, on the plea, stated in an official letter, that "every reasonable facility had been afforded for criticism." A respectful letter of remonstrance was forwarded by him to the Marquis of Lothian. Its style of formal courtesy would suggest that it had been drawn up more probably by some legal member of the council of the Cockburn Association, and sent to him for signature. But having done so, his own simple and plain-spoken style is unmistakably manifest in the postscript he has added: "The proposed designs, I can assure you, will give great dissatisfaction. They are not at all in keeping with the grand old Castle."

CHAPTER XIII.

HOME HOLIDAYS.

THE recreations of each summer's holiday alternated between foreign travel through unfamiliar scenes, and a sojourn in some choice centre of Scottish scenery and historical associations. But it was indispensable for William Nelson's full enjoyment of either that it should be shared with Mrs. Nelson and his children. Indeed, the hints that occasionally transpire in his letters, of the pleasure with which he exchanged their summer resort for Salisbury Green and Parkside, show that he had been thinking far more of their happiness than his own. He liked his children to travel, and while they were still young repeatedly sent them abroad, either with a tutor and governess, or under the care of some trusted friend. He had a strong prejudice against Continental boarding-schools, and instead of sending his daughters to one, he preferred arranging for their spending successive winters abroad in charge of a friend, where they had the advantage of masters who came daily to them. The same feeling animated him in later years, alike in his plans for foreign travel, and in the choice of a summer haunt among favourite Scottish scenery.

Of the latter, pleasant memories come back to me of many a ramble by the Tweed and its tributaries the Ettrick, the Leader, the Yarrow, and other haunted streams; and by St. Mary's Loch, which has wooed alike the poets of elder and of modern times. A mere residence in the country, however attractive the scenery might be, speedily proved irksome to William Nelson. His active mind required constant occupation; and the physical impediments which increasing obesity, accompanied by a retarded action of the heart, interposed in the way of long pedestrian excursions, only led to a change in the methods of attaining the same end. He was ever on the look-out for some fresh and unfamiliar scene. In the summer of 1879 he made his way to St. Kilda, a curious little, outlying, ocean-girt rock of the Hebrides, the only one of a lonely group that is inhabited—

" Nature's last limit, hemmed with ocean round."

Its population numbered in all seventy-five, a decrease from the previous year; for, as one of them said, "they had lost a foine woman, the only one who coot speak Enklish." The rude little hamlet, with its primitive stone dwellings, each of two apartments, attracted Mr. Nelson's curious study; and beyond it a no less primitive bit of masonry incovered the Tober Childa Chalda, or St. Kilda's Well, by the village. But this visit to St. Kilda is noticeable here for an incident associated with one of William Nelson's peculiarities that bordered on eccentricity. Though a business man of punctual habits, and exacting habitual punctuality in others, he never carried a watch, and indeed, I believe, never possessed one. He had some inexplicable way of guessing the time, and could tell it generally with wonderful approach to accuracy. He never missed a train, or failed to keep an appointment, and could not see what people wanted with watches. He said he did perfectly well without one. But this St. Kilda trip furnished an occasion when, for once, he deplored the want of a timepiece. Immediately on landing on the island the party were met by the minister, who eagerly inquired if any of them had a watch, to tell him what o'clock it was. It turned out, on inquiry, that the minister's watch, which was the only one on the island, had been sent away for repair six months before; and if William Nelson had been the fortunate possessor of one, here was an opportunity for its useful disposal.

The following summer was passed at Philiphaugh, rich in memories of Montrose and Leslie; of Alison Rutherford, the songstress; of Scott, sheriff, as well as poet and novelist; of Hogg, Wordsworth, and all the legends of the Dowie Dens of Yarrow. The river famed in song and story flowed by near the house, with "the Duchess's Walk," a charming wooded path on the opposite bank of the river, leading through the grounds of Bowhill to Newark Castle. Kirkhope Tower, Branksome Hall, Melrose Abbey, and many another hoary pile, were within reach. William Nelson's memory was stored with passages from his favourite poets; and as the associations of the scene called them to remembrance, he would repeat long pieces suggested by the locality or adapted to it. It is the centre of old traditions of the Flodden men; and many a spot along the Tweed and its tributaries tempted us each new day to wander through scenes that told everywhere of the Last Minstrel and his Lay. In a letter to Mr. Campbell he says: "I write this at Philiphaugh, a mansion that we have taken for summer quarters. It is about two miles from Selkirk, the scene of the defeat of the Marquis of Montrose. The estate is still owned by the Murrays of Philiphaugh, the same family who have held it since the old times of the Border raids and the Debatable Land. A cairn near the house, now overgrown with ivy, is said to mark the spot where the Highlanders were surprised by Leslie, and the Marquis turned and fled. A stone on the cairn is inscribed, 'To the memory of the Covenanters who fought and fell on the field of Philiphaugh, and won the battle there, A.D. September 13,

1645.' The grounds and woods are extensive and **fine**;
and there is good fishing for Fred, as the Yarrow and
the Ettrick are close at hand; and there will be good
shooting for him when the time comes......We had Dr.
and Mrs. Wilson and their daughter with us lately.
We enjoyed their visit much; and oh! how fond Dr.
Wilson is of Auld Reekie and its associations, though,
alas, there is but little left now of the ancient city."

Again, in the summer of 1883 came a concise message by ocean cable, followed by the ampler invitation:
" I have taken Cowdenknowes for the summer. Come
and let us have a look at its surroundings; do not fail.
Cowdenknowes, I may tell you, is an old mansion, historically interesting, which is situated in one of the
most lovely districts in the south of Scotland. It is
about five miles from Melrose; and the remains of the
castle of Thomas the Rhymer, which consist of very
picturesque ivy-covered walls, are on the property.
The Leader passes through the grounds, and it is an
excellent trouting-stream. It has already been laid
under contribution in this way by Professor Annandale and Fred, whenever the water was in a good state
for the rod." Here, as at Philiphaugh, some fresh
ramble was planned each morning; while the evenings
were beguiled with pleasant converse, and apt quotations germane to the scenes of that land of romance.
The ruined castle of Thomas of Ercildoun has already

been noted as close by. In a neighbouring valley was Oakwood Tower, of old the dwelling of the wondrous Michael Scott,—

> " A wizard of such dreaded fame,
>   That when in Salamanca's cave
>   Him listed his magic wand to wave,
>   The bells would ring in Notre Dame."

The Eildon Hills, the tokens of his power, and Melrose, where his bones were laid " on St. Michael's night," are only a few miles off.   The picturesque ruin of Smailholme Tower, where the later minstrel spent the happiest days of his childhood, was within reach; Abbotsford, the Fairy Dean, and the Rhymer's Glen, Dryburgh, and the vale of Tweed, haunted at every winding with some old tale or song, all wooed us by turns.   So each day had its excursion, its legend of some sort to investigate, its ruin to explore.   It was with William Nelson on the Tweed as on the Nile: he was indefatigable in the pursuit of information concerning every minutest object of interest, and never was satisfied till he had seen for himself, and questioned and sifted all available evidence.   The memories of many a pleasant day, with the incidents of kindly intercourse and genial humour that added fresh sunshine to the scene, would furnish material enough to add many a chapter over which old friends would not readily tire.   But such reminiscences can only be glanced at

here. I select, therefore, from among those home holidays the latest of all: a summer at Glenfeochan.

Glenfeochan is a romantic glen of the West Highlands, through which the Feochan finds its way to the
sea. Oban is only six miles off, and so steamers and
boats and all the attractions of the sea are at hand,
such as ever had a fascination for William Nelson. For
he guessed, as has been seen, that could the pedigree
of the Nelsons of Throsk be followed up, they might
prove to be of the stock of old Danish rovers, the
sons of Thor, whose home was on the sea; and so he
welcomed the hint at an etymology of the Bannockburn
farm from the Thor of the Vikings. Unquestionably
he possessed not a little of their steady hardihood and
love of adventure, softened though it was by trans-
mission through a sober race of Covenanters, who tilled
the carse where Bruce had triumphed, and, when needs
were, could emulate him in sturdy resistance to the
tyrant.

Glenfeochan House is beautifully situated at the foot
of the glen. It lies low—perhaps a little too low—
nestling among the hills, with glens and lochs on every
hand. The drawing-room windows looked across the
river to the sea; and when the curtains were drawn,
and a fire was found not unpleasant in the cool autumn
evenings, the emotional delight with which William
Nelson welcomed the songs of Scotland, or some of his

favourite hymns, was infectious. His taste in music
was simple, but it yielded him intense pleasure, and
not infrequently moved him to tears. But such evening relaxations were generally the close of a busy day;
for Oban is a choice centre for the explorer. It afforded
means of access to the fiords or sea-lochs of Argyleshire,
and to the outlying Hebrides. There were Iona and
Staffa, Glencoe and Mull, with the ruined keep of
Duart Castle, the Lady Rock, and the legend of "Fair
Ellen of Lorne," which is perpetuated in Campbell's
ballad of "Glenara." There was the vitrified fort of
Dun MacUisneachan at Loch Etive to explore; and on
the opposite side of the loch, Dunstaffnage, the home of
the Dalriadic kings, where of old was held in safe keeping the *liah fhail*, or stone of destiny, now enshrined in
the coronation chair in Westminster Abbey. The unique
cairn or serpent-mound of Loch Nell, another object of
special curiosity, was visited more than once, in the
hope of arriving at some definite idea of its actual
character. For the fact of a huge saurian mound, like
some of those in the valley of the Ohio, lying there in
a secluded nook between the hills of Lorne that form
the steep escarpment of Glenfeochan, was a thing too
exceptional for William Nelson to allow to pass without some attempt at a solution of its mysteries.

But the choicest of that summer's explorations was
a day on Eilean Naombh, or Holy Island. Our High-

land boatmen called it Oil Tsiach n'an Naombh (the College of the Holy People), if we understood rightly; for we had a good deal more Gaelic than tended to our illumination. Our party was pleasantly augmented by the addition of the Rev. Dr. Walter Smith; and William Nelson's sense of humour was keenly excited by his report of a dialogue between two of the Highlanders, who, happily for us, spoke in English. "James," said the younger of the two, "I have been told that when the deceiver tempted our mother Eve, it was in Gaelic that he spoke."—"Well, Donald, I should think it not at all improbable. The Gaelic is a very sweet and persuasive language, particularly when well spoken!" The idea that the Devil's Gaelic must necessarily be of the best, was a subject of much mirthful comment. Holy Island, the southernmost of the Garvelloch Isles, lies opposite Scarba, with the famous whirlpool of Corryvrechan between. The landing is in a deep cove, where the first object of attraction is St. Columba's Well, a clear fountain of fresh water bubbling out of the living rock on the margin of the sea. A flight of steps leads up from the sacred pool; and on a level area a short way above stands the chapel of St. Columba, a little ruined cell of only twenty-one feet long. It is of the most primitive Celtic type. A narrow, square-headed opening in the east end, deeply splayed externally, constitutes the east window; under which is the

simple altar-slab of slate, still entire. On a neighbouring height a rude enclosure, marked by an upright stone
with an incised cross, is traditionally known as the
grave of St. Eithne, the mother of St. Columba. But
the special objects we were in search of were a pair
of bee-hive houses, which we found not far from the
chapel. They are built of unhewed slabs, without
cement, conjoined like a figure ∞, rude as any Hot-
tentot kraal, and old, probably, as the days of the
sainted missionary's first sojourn among the pagan
Celts. The little island is uninhabited, and out of the
reach of ordinary tourists, so that time and weather
are the only injurers of its curious relics. The day at
Holy Island was one of rare enjoyment to all, but
especially to William Nelson, whose intelligent inquisi-
tiveness and love of adventure were equally gratified.

Within more easy reach of Glenfeochan, in a sequestered nook among the hills, lies the ancient cemetery
of Kilbride, with its ruined church, its holy well, and
moss-grown sepulchral memorials. Here, among others
of note in the district, lie the Macdougals of Lorne,
whose castle of Dunolly stands at the mouth of
Oban Bay, with their more modern mansion near by,
where is still preserved the famous Brooch of Lorne.
But here, above all, lies prostrate, in three detached
pieces, a singularly beautiful sculptured cross, with a
figure of the crucifixion, and the traces that show where

a crown of bronze, or other more precious metal, surrounded the Saviour's head. Its inscription was conned
and puzzled over in repeated visits. Rubbings were
taken of it, and the legend at length deciphered, showing that it was erected in 1616 by the lord of the
neighbouring manor, Alexander Campbell of Laeraig.

The Cross of Kilbride had at this time an unwonted
interest, for William Nelson was already enlisted in the
project of erecting at Kinghorn a memorial cross to
Alexander III., the last of the Celtic kings, in the successful accomplishment of which, as will be seen hereafter, he took an active part. But, meanwhile, some
of the Glenfeochan experiences of a more special character are worth noting. A letter that followed me to
Canada, written in the middle of October, supplies the
details. "Our stay at Glenfeochan," he writes, " is
fast drawing to a close, Fred only remaining behind
till the end of the week, unless great success with his
rod should tempt him to stay longer. The sight of
Loch Nell on Friday last made his teeth water, as
salmon were leaping in it at the north end in great
numbers ; he is sure he saw at least forty of them so
engaged. He was not rewarded, however, with even
a rise from any of them, and he had to be contented
with bringing home nothing but a single sea-trout,
which, however, was a very respectable one as to size,
and in splendid condition......There was very nearly

being a terrible tragedy here, the story of which is this. We had staying with us a son of Mr. Keeley Halswell, the artist, a boy of eleven years of age. He made friends with the son of the gardener, a boy about eight; and the two went one day to the loft over the stable to catch mice, they being accompanied by Bertram's little dog, Gip. There is in the loft a large chest for holding grain for the horses, but it was empty at the time; and what did the two little fellows do? They lifted up the lid and got into the chest, in order that they might not be seen by the mice; and down came the lid, the catch took hold, and they were imprisoned like poor Ginevra of Rogers's 'Italy,'—

> ' When a spring-lock that lay in ambush there
> Fastened them down,'

but happily not for ever. They made what noise they could, and Bertram heard this; but he thought it was just the boys amusing themselves, and so he paid no attention to it. Thus it went on, and the poor little fellows so suffered from want of fresh air that they could not speak to each other, and were getting very faint. Young Halswell had a dreadful headache; when at what would have been in all likelihood their last effort, they tried the lid of the chest, and found to their surprise that it opened, and they were free, after a confinement that must have lasted about three hours.

For their release they were indebted to the little dog Gip. After the lid came down they heard the little creature running round the chest and leaping on it in a state of great excitement, as if conscious that there was something wrong. His leaps were continued for a long time; and they are sure that in one of them he must have pushed his nose at the hasp of the lid and opened it, and hence their release. Well done, Gip! Nothing could have been more extraordinary or more unexpected than this." In the same letter he refers to a robbery that had just taken place at Parkside, by which about £250 had been carried off out of the safe. The police seemed to think that the robbery might have been committed by some one in the works. It was amusingly characteristic of the writer to find him in a subsequent letter seemingly deriving much satisfaction from the fact that the rogue had not been convicted!

His recreations, as already stated, alternated between such pleasant rambles among the beauties of nature and objects of historic and archæological interest in his own country as have been glanced at here, and a journey through novel scenes in foreign lands. The previous summer had been devoted to the tour in the Baltic and Russia, which has furnished some brief notes for a previous chapter. Writing to his friend, Major MacEnery, soon after his return, Mr. Nelson thus indicated the plans he was already maturing for another season : "We went over a good many thousand miles in our late journeyings. The only breakdown was that of Florence, at Moscow, which came in the way to prevent our all going to the Volga, and seeing some of the strange sights that are to be witnessed there, especially at the great fair of Nijni-Novgorod. So we had to leave our visit to that part of the world till another opportunity ; and when I go next to Moscow, which I hope will be in the course of next summer or autumn, if all's well, I will not be satisfied unless I go down the Volga to Astrakhan, at the extreme north of the Caspian Sea, and sail down that sea to Baku, where the celebrated oil wells are, and take the railway then across to Batoum on the Black Sea, and go thence to the Crimea, and so find my way home by Greece and Vienna : and this will be a glorious journey."

With such visions of future journeyings in strange lands the year 1884 had drawn to a close. The "breakdown at Moscow," referred to above, though it so far balked the plans of the travellers, does not appear to have materially lessened the pleasure of their trip. In a letter of Mr. Simon Fraser MacLeod, I find allusions only to "our visit to this delightful and picturesque old city of Moscow." The view of it from the Kremlin surpassed in its novel and singularly picturesque aspect anything ever seen by them before. They saw also

a no less novel illustration of sacred art, thus described
by the same young traveller: "The Church of the
Assumption is a golden pile assuredly; and besides the
head of a nail from the true cross, and a portion of the
Virgin's mantle, it contains a sacred painting by St.
Luke, the beloved physician. He may have excelled
in his latter profession; but prepared as we were to find
any merits in his painting of the holy mother, we could
not discover even the lines of a face or any pretence
of a likeness possible through the rawness of the
colours used by the evangelist in those early and
primitive days of art. Mr. Nelson, by the aid of a
candle dimly burning, thought at one time he had discovered something resembling a beautiful face; but on
my suggesting that it was but the reflection of his own
expressive features that he saw, we came to the conclu-
sion that such was the actual state of the matter." All
was novel, interesting, and delightful; for the tour was
to prove for two bright young members of the party
the prelude to their joining hand in hand to enter
together on the journey of life. They shared in the
Glenfeochan holiday of the following summer, where
their own final arrangements were settled, to the satisfaction of all; and so with pleasant memories and
brightest hopes the family gathered once more round
the cheerful hearth of Salisbury Green.

CHAPTER XIV.

PROJECTED TRAVEL—THE END.

THE route from Oban to Edinburgh passes through some of the most beautiful and romantic scenes of Scottish landscape : by the Pass of Brander, Loch Awe, St. Fillans, and Doune Castle, to Stirling ; and then by Bannockburn, the Strath of Falkirk, and the old Nelson homestead of Throsk, to "the gray metropolis of the north." After a few days or weeks of zealous exploration around Glenfeochan, or off to neighbouring islands and more distant glens, in the fashion already described, a run into Edinburgh was a welcome change. There William Nelson was equally at home when making a pleasure of business or a business of his most favourite pleasures.

The city, built on the picturesque heights surrounding the Castle Rock, embosomed among hills, and looking out on the sea, has a singular fascination for its citizens ; and with William Nelson it was a passion, like that of the old Hebrew for Jerusalem, or the Athenian for the City of the Violet Crown. The

Cockburn Association, which has already been referred to, takes its name from Lord Cockburn, the friend of Scott, of Brougham, and Jeffrey; the enthusiastic advocate of whatever tended to protect the historical remains and to preserve the beauty of their native city; and the mantle of the genial old judge seemed to have been bequeathed to William Nelson, with a double portion of his spirit. As an active member of the council of the association, his zeal in protesting against every piece of tasteless vandalism was unremitting. But his enthusiasm would not allow him to be content with mere wishes or denouncements. He had the means as well as the will, and when civic officials and Government functionaries dallied and disputed over needful reforms, he took them in hand himself, on a scale of liberality all the more admirable from the genuine modesty which repelled all public recognition. And yet evidence survives to show how far his aims exceeded even his own comprehensive liberality.

With the fancy that begot for Edinburgh in the heyday of its literary glory the name of the Modern Athens, there grew up in the minds of a past generation the idea of rearing on the Calton Hill, as a modern Acropolis, a reproduction of the Parthenon, with, it is to be presumed, the sculptures of some Scottish Phidias as its final adornment. It was to constitute a sacred Pantheon, in special commemoration of those to whom the nation owed the welcome boon of an honourable peace after the protracted strife of the Napoleonic wars. In old school-boy days it had been a matter of liveliest interest to watch the process of construction that promised the accomplishment of this ambitious scheme. One after another, the lofty Doric columns rose to the number of twelve; and then the work stopped. The builders had neglected the wise maxim to sit down first and count the cost, whether they had sufficient means to finish it. The funds had given out at that early stage. The boys that had watched the first efforts of its builders grew gray with years; and the abortive Parthenon—a monument of ambitious folly—became familiar to the eyes of a new generation, till they ceased to realize its absurdity. There were indeed men of taste whom it continued to offend. David Roberts, himself a native of Edinburgh, and with the keen eye of an artist for architectural effect, was loath to abandon the dream of a new Parthenon. The late D. R. Hay, the ingenious author of " The Laws of Harmonious Colouring" and " The Natural Principles of the Harmony of Form," united with James Ballantyne, the poet, and a little band of kindred spirits, in a vain effort to revive the scheme. But the later Renaissance had died out. The taste of the age had reverted once more to mediæval art, and their exertions proved fruitless. William Nelson thoroughly appreciated the absurdity of this gigantic failure. With grim mirth he satirized the builders who had made such a beginning and were not able to finish. But he did not despair of seeing even that huge blot erased; and in May 1887, while busy with his Castle and other restorations, he thus wrote in a letter intended for his friend Dr. Field, but which was found among his papers, unfinished, after his death : "Here is a matter that I have been thinking of for some time ; and in case you may think that I am off the rails in regard to it mentally, I have to say, 'I am not mad, most noble Festus ; I speak the words of truth and soberness.' You will be aware that it was intended, a great many years ago, that there should be a building on the Calton Hill here, which would be a facsimile of the Parthenon at Athens, and twelve pillars which were intended for the portico of the building were erected. But there were no funds to go further ; and the pillars in consequence stand, as it were, a monument of Scottish folly. Now it would be a grand thing, not only for Edinburgh, but for Scotland generally, if the building were completed, and were made a Walhalla for statues and busts of Scotchmen who have distinguished themselves in the service of their country and otherwise ; and it would be all the better if the completion of the building were to be made an international object. Now I know that your worthy brother, Cyrus Field, likes to do things that are international, and I will take it kind if you will have a talk with him on this subject; and if he will open his purse and give a grand contribution towards the completion of what would be a truly noble building, I would get the matter started." He then goes into a calculation of the cost. He had consulted with an architect, who estimated the necessary sum as not less than £150,000. He then goes on to say: " I send you a photograph of the poor shivering pillars that have been erected; and I hope that there is spirit enough among moneyed men in America and Scotland not to allow them to stand much longer in their solitary condition." A blank in the letter shows that some estimated item had yet to be ascertained; and so the letter lay unfinished and unsent.

It is thus apparent that there were scarcely any limits to his ideal of the Edinburgh of the future. The maintenance of his native city in unblemished honour and beauty was the source of many a fascinating dream, and took form at times in the union of such idealizations with his practical liberality. Hence the desertion of the Highlands for the city was no exchange of the poetry of life for mere prosaic realities. Edinburgh was rich in all the materials wherewith to fashion an ever-new romance: a thing of beauty to be preserved or to be made more beautiful. There the landscape gardener, the architect, and decorator, were all busily at work on his plans for renovating St. Bernard's Well. The sculptor's studio had to be visited to learn of the progress of the new statue. Then, too, official formalities and obstructions had at length yielded to his quiet persistency, and the plans were in progress for restorations, not only on the great hall of the Castle, but also on the Argyle Tower, and the venerable little oratory known as St. Margaret's Chapel. With the latter object in view, more than one excursion had been made to Iona, where the little Norman structure styled the Chapel of St. Oran is affirmed to have been built by St. Margaret, the queen of Malcolm Canmore. Hence it was assumed to furnish the fittest model for a design to replace the somewhat commonplace modern restoration of the original doorway. A photograph of it was accordingly secured, and placed, for that purpose, in the architect's hands.

The Argyle Tower, of old the state prison, was to be freed from manifold incongruities of modern barbarism, as has since been done in the best taste. But William Nelson's sympathies were not narrowed within the bounds of his native city, and a special occasion now invited his practical co-operation elsewhere. The approaching anniversary of the death of the good king Alexander III., last and best of Scotland's Celtic kings, was to be signalized by the erection of a memorial cross to mark the scene of that fatal event of six centuries before, the fruits of which are bewailed in the fine old fragment of native elegy preserved for us in Wyntoun's Chronicles, the earliest known lyric in the Scottish language. The old chronicler pictures the prosperity of the nation under the rule of him that led Scotland in love and loyalty; and then he says,—

> " This failèd fra he died suddenly;
>   This sang was made of him forthi:
> When Alexander our king was dead,
>   That Scotland led in love and lea,
> Away wes söns of ale and bread,
>   Of wine and wax, of gaming and glee;
> Our gold was changèd into lead.
>   Christ, born into virginity,
> Succor Scotland and remede
>   That stad is in perplexity."

Kinghorn, the birthplace of William Nelson's mother, and the scene of many of the happiest days of his own childhood and youth, was the place historically associated with the national disaster. When he carried off his sisters to revisit the old scenes, it will be remembered that one of the special spots pointed out to them was "The King's Crag," as the point is called which tradition assigns as the actual cliff over which, when his horse stumbled, Alexander III. was precipitated. The event was thus associated with many of William Nelson's earliest recollections; and the proposal to mark it with a suitable monument was responded to by him with hearty enthusiasm. From its initiation his zeal never flagged. First came his subscription, the most liberal of all; then correspondence and deliberations as to the design, the inscription, the most durable and best material. He writes to the Rev. Charles Shaw from Glenfeochan in October 1886, in reference to the appeal for subscriptions:—"Let me know as soon as you can what is the result, and I will then see what I can do to make up the sum." In December he discusses the details of the design and material. He fears, from its exposed site on the highroad from Burntisland to Kinghorn, that the monument will be liable to injury; has "called the architect Mr. Blanc's attention some time ago to this circumstance, and that he ought not to forget it in making his finished drawings." Again he writes in the following February:—"Mr. Blanc says that the memorial cross ought decidedly to be of Peterhead granite; and you will please hold me responsible for whatever shortcoming there may be in consequence." Then comes an equally characteristic passage: "I don't think there is any occasion for you or Dr. Rogers telling the committee of what you call my handsome offer. If this were done, the matter would, I have no doubt, be blazoned forth in the newspapers, and I would not like that at all." The next proposition was that he should unveil the monument, in the erection of which he had manifested so practical an interest. But that he would not hear of, and suggested the Earl of Elgin as Lord

Lieutenant of the county, and a good man to boot. "Failing him, you should apply to Lord Napier and Ettrick, or Lord Rosebery."

When at length the memorable day arrived, there was not only the beautiful memorial cross to unveil, but a new public park and golfing ground to open. The authorities of the ancient burgh would not be balked of their wish to mark in some way their sense of Mr. Nelson's generous co-operation in the work, so Lord Elgin and he were both admitted to all the honours and privileges of burgesses of Kinghorn. The speech of the latter, in reply to the provost's address in handing to him his burgess ticket, is too replete with characteristic feeling and personal reminiscences to be omitted here. He was no orator, and indeed shrank with instinctive reserve from all public appearances; but the simple utterances of genuine feeling are the best of all oratory.

"Fortunately for myself," he said, "and perhaps still more fortunately for those who hear me, I am not often in circumstances which call upon me to speak in public. On the present occasion, when there has been conferred on me the high honour of being made a burgess of the royal burgh of Kinghorn—an honour which I never expected, and which I do not feel that I have done anything to merit—for this, gentlemen, I thank you most sincerely. It is an honour which shall ever be held by

me, and by those who come after me, in the highest
esteem. There are many things which make Kinghorn
a place of much interest to me, and which give a peculiar
value to any mark of respect which comes from its
town council or its inhabitants. For one thing, it was
the birthplace of my mother, and we all know what
that means. But it must not be supposed that my
attachment to Kinghorn is solely on this account. I
love it for its own sake, for its quaint and picturesque
old character as a royal burgh; and I love it also for
its fine coast-scenery, with its beautiful sands, its bold
rocks, and its many advantages for bathing, fishing,
and even for those who think they perform their whole
duty at the seaside when they merely saunter along
it and inhale its health-giving breezes. But I love it
still more—perhaps most of all—for the sunshine with
which it filled my early years, making my holidays
holidays indeed. I stayed always with my grandfather
and grandmother, whose kindness was very great and
unceasing. So strong was the impression made upon
me at that early period of my life, that I never allow a
season to pass without visiting Kinghorn, and renewing
my acquaintance with the rocky scenery of the coast,
which must be admitted to be exceptionally fine. So
great is my familiarity with the coast here that I know
every rock of any consequence that it contains; and I
may add that there are few places more richly endowed

with all the amenities which health-seekers are in quest
of and value.   It ought to be one of the most popular
of the health-resorts on our shores.   Another thing
which took a hold of me in my early years, and which
I still remember well, was the talk of the old folks.
They had some themes on which they never ceased to
descant.   One of these was Paul Jones's piratical visit
to the Firth of Forth, which was looked upon as a very
formidable event by the small towns on the coast of
Fife, but which happily turned out a scare.   My grandmother saw the big ship of the pirate from near the
hamlet of Glassmount, about two miles from Kinghorn.   And there is good news for strangers who may
come now-a-days to the old place for summer quarters.
They need not be afraid for another Paul Jones coming
to alarm them, as there is now a strong fortress on the
Pettycur road, under the shadow of whose wings they
may rest in perfect safety.   But there was another
matter quite as engrossing, and that was the injury
which steam-boats had done or would do to the town.
Before these began to ply there were big, ordinary boats
which carried passengers ; and as these boats started
only at particular times of the tide, passengers had
generally to stay some time in the town : more to the
delight of the innkeepers and others, we should imagine,
than to that of the strangers thus detained, in order to
have the opportunity of leaving a little of their money

behind them. We know better now; and I am sure that the inhabitants of Kinghorn would not be inclined to go back, on any terms whatever, to those good old ways, so easy in all that belonged to them. Such retrospects, while both interesting and instructive, are not without an infusion of sadness. In my case, early companions in and about Kinghorn have all disappeared but two : namely, Henry Darney, a worthy citizen of the town, and Major Greig, now of Toronto, Canada. It is a touching thought, and brings to my remembrance the tender and beautiful verses of Delta, with which I conclude :—

> ' Where are the playmates of those years?
>   Hills arise and oceans roll between.
> We call, but scarcely one appears ;
>   No more shall be what once has been.
>
> ' Yet, gazing o'er the bleak green sea,
>   O'er snow-capped cliffs and desert plain,
> Mirrored in thought methinks to me
>   The spectral past returns again.
>
> ' Once more to retrospection's eyes,
>   As 'twere to present life restored,
> The perished and the past arise,
>   The early lost and long deplored.' "

While the memorial cross erected on the King's Crag had been thus occupying so much of his attention, the various works of restoration undertaken by him in

Edinburgh were not neglected. They continued, indeed to engage his attention, and to furnish him with ever-renewed pleasure, till the close of his life. He thus writes to me in April 1887:—"St. Bernard's Well is not quite finished yet, but it begins to look very different from what you will remember of it in our morning visits together: quite a little gem indeed, now that the mosaic work is done, or nearly so. A handsome parapet wall with railing runs along the river-side. The grounds are laid out, I think, in good taste, and a fine broad stair leads down from the street instead of the dingy back way you and I used to have to traverse in our morning visits to the well. Altogether it is a great success. The number of visitors to the well has greatly increased already; and if it correspondingly diminishes the number of visitors to the taverns, as I hope it will, then we have all the success that could be desired. You must repeat your visit to us soon, and have another tumbler of the water, and see all we have been doing in the way of improvement; it will be all in order before you arrive."

Again, in a postscript to one of his letters to the Rev. Charles Shaw, in the early part of the same year, he says: "My restorations at the Castle are getting on briskly. The Argyle Tower is far advanced, and as a piece of architecture it will be a great success. The hospital building has been made over to me, and operations for the restoration and conversion of it into what will be almost a facsimile of the old Parliament Hall have been already begun. It will be a very interesting building in its reformed condition." In another letter to the same correspondent, who was an active member of the local committee for the erection of the memorial cross at Kinghorn, he thus writes:—" I send you a letter that I received a few days ago from Lord Napier. I asked him if he would come to the unveiling of the memorial to Alexander III., and let his voice be heard on the occasion as one of the speakers; but this, he says, he will be unable to do. The first part of the letter is of special interest to you, as it refers to some discoveries that have been made at the clearing out of the old Parliament Hall in the Castle. They have been so important that an almost perfect facsimile can be made of the hall as it was in the days of its glory: all except in the matter of the tapestry with which the walls were either wholly or partly covered; and it would be too much to hope for that any part of this should be to the fore at this time of day. Everything else is known. The roof exists in its entirety; parts of the floor have been found. It was of Arbroath pavement; and the account for the freight of the stones from Dundee to Leith has been recovered in the Rolls of the Exchequer in the Register Office. The ancient windows have also been discovered,

and they just require to be cleared of the masonry
with which they have been built up, and have fresh
mullions inserted; and it is known how the original
mullions would be from specimens that exist in other
buildings of the period. The doorway that formed the
ancient main entrance to the building has been found.
The doorway and stair that led to the kitchen, which
was below the hall, have also been discovered; and the
kitchen exists in its entirety, it being made use of as
a store for clothing for the troops. From the great
size of it and that of the fireplace, it is clear that
creature comforts were not overlooked in days of yore
by our old Scottish legislators."

Public interest grew apace as the work of restoration
in the Castle progressed. The Argyle Tower, as it
approached completion, presented an attractive feature,
harmonizing admirably with the older remains of the
fortress, and attracting the notice of all, as seen from
Princes Street. As the rumour of one after another of
the discoveries of original portions of the great hall,
furnishing valuable guidance for its restoration, gained
currency, fresh zest was given to public curiosity. Paragraphs, such as the one quoted below, made their appearance from time to time in the daily press, until a
general interest was revived, and a renewed anxiety
expressed, not only for completing the restoration of
the ancient buildings, but for making such modifica-

tions of the huge, unsightly pile of barracks and other modern structures within the Castle as should make them harmonize in some degree with its ancient features.

" Yesterday afternoon the Marquis of Lothian, along with Mr. William Nelson, drove up to Edinburgh Castle and examined the alterations which are being carried out there at the expense of the latter. The work of clearing out the old Parliament Hall is proceeding apace. Finely-carved, and in most cases well-preserved, freestone corbels have been uncovered underneath the plaster. In no two cases are the designs on these corbels alike. In one it is a lion's head, in another a thistle, in a third a rose, a fourth is a female head, while others bear the letters I.R., and I.H.S., the former evidently meant for 'James Rex.' At the north-eastern corner of the hall, the top of a staircase which apparently must have led from ' the Queen Mary ' apartments in the Palace to the balcony outside the Parliament Hall, has been discovered; but it is not yet known at what point in the royal apartments the lower end of the staircase came out. The restoration of the Argyle Tower is rapidly approaching completion, and the masons are now engaged in building the hewn stones on the roof."

One result of all this was that Mr. Nelson responded to the intelligent interest manifested in the work now in progress by arranging for a succession of Saturday visits to the Castle. I am indebted to an old friend, who shared in the pleasure of those informal gatherings, for the following account of them: "They were attended by artists and antiquaries, professors from the University, and literary men; to whom were added occasionally some distinguished stranger, as well as officers of rank who felt a professional interest in the work. Along with those were always to be seen some of the clerks and workmen from Parkside; and it was very pleasant to notice the kind way in which he made them feel at their ease, and indeed seemed totally unconscious of anything unusual, as he turned from some learned professor or officer of rank to address himself with marked respect to one of his own employés, and explain to him the significance of some recently disclosed portions of the original building."

Meanwhile the grand scheme of a tour by the Volga to Astrakhan, and by the Caspian Sea and the overland route to Batoum on the Black Sea, and so to Greece, had been first delayed, and then greatly modified. In the midst of all this preoccupation with mediæval restorations in his own romantic town, he turned anew to the favourite classical studies of early years; and his letters in the spring and summer of 1886 show that Hellenic history, and the associations that linger around every cape and mountain, river and vale of Greece, had quickened into an intense longing to explore their storied scenery. In the month of August 1887, I was off on a holiday ramble in the White Mountains—the Highlands of New England—where a letter followed me, the last I was ever to receive from my oldest surviving friend. "I intend," he wrote, "to set out on a trip to Greece about the middle of next month, taking with me a party which will consist of Mrs. Nelson, Meta, Alice, and Dr. Walter Smith, who will act as chaplain. We will go direct to Trieste from London, *via* Dover, Calais, Basle, and Venice; and will sail for Athens by the Austrian Lloyd's steamer which leaves on Saturday, the 24th, for the Piræus; a voyage which will occupy about three and a half days. After spending a fortnight there, we will likely, if all is well, push on for Constantinople; and after being there for about a week, will return home as rapidly as possible. Such at least is my present intention, and I trust that nothing will occur to prevent my carrying out the programme." He then gives an account of the successful completion of the work at St. Bernard's Well, and thus proceeds: "As to the Castle, the Argyle Tower is finished, and it forms a striking object viewed from Princes Street, and is a great improvement to the outline of the north side of the Castle. The architect deserves great praise for having done his part so well in the restoration of this building. The room that is above what was the old state prison is a very fine one, and the feeling of the architecture of the period that he has aimed at—which is, if I remember right, about the year 1500—is admirably carried out. The room, when I get it hung round with engravings of the Castle at different periods from 1573 downwards, and also get it decorated in various parts with trophies of arms and armour, which I am to have permission to select from the armoury in the Castle, will be one of the most interesting rooms there. My collection of views of the Castle will be largely taken advantage of for the decoration of this room. The view from the top of the tower is, I need not say, one of the finest in Europe; and there is a path right round, so that the view can be seen from all points.

"The old Parliament Hall has been at a stand-still for some time; but Mr. Blanc has drawings for the windows and doors completed, and estimates for them are now being taken. Here is a point on which I would like to be enlightened. You say in your 'Memorials of Edinburgh:' 'From the occasional assembling of the Parliament here, while the Scottish monarchs continued to reside in the Castle, it still retains the name of the Parliament House.' Now at a gathering of eminent men of Edinburgh that I had at the Castle some time ago, Mr. Dickson of the antiquarian department of the Register Office took it upon him to give an address to the party when they

were in the said hall; and he said in the course of it
that it was quite a misnomer to connect the word
parliament with the building, as the old Scottish Parliament met in the Tolbooth, and there does not exist
any evidence to show that any of its meetings were
ever held in the old Parliament Hall. What do you
say to this, my dear old fellow? A few lines about
the matter by return of mail from you will be a
favour. By the way, a discovery has been made lately
in regard to the building which will interest you. It
is that the walls are much older than the corbels, the
latter having been found to have been stuck into them:
Mr. Blanc is of opinion about two hundred years after
they were built. What do you say to this discovery?"

I was out of the reach of mails, as well as of books;
and so August had passed into September ere an
answer could be penned to the above queries. "The
hall," as I wrote in reply, "was undoubtedly the great
banquet-hall of the Castle, where, when the king resided there, he occupied the daïs, along with the nobles
in attendance, while inferior guests and retainers sat
at the table below. But such halls were available for
any large assembly; and in truth Scotland had no
regular Parliament House till the reign of Charles I.
Old Parliaments for the most part followed the Court,
and found a place for meeting as they best could—in the
hall of some great abbey or royal castle; or failing either,

in a church or town hall. When, for example, Philip IV. of France quarrelled with the Pope in 1302, the only place of meeting that Paris could furnish for the States General was the church of Notre Dame. When the English Court was at Westminster, the Parliament turned St. Stephen's Chapel to like account; and the Blackfriars' Monastery at Perth, in all probability, afforded the usual place of meeting for the Scottish Parliament, till the assassination of James I. in 1437 led to the transference of the Court to Edinburgh, with a view doubtless to safe royal residence within the Castle. Only one **Parliament**, the thirteenth of his reign, met at Edinburgh, in what hall is not specified. But, immediately after the death of the poet-king, the first **Parliament of the** new reign assembled there; and the record for once leaves no doubt. It runs thus: ʻQuo die comparentibus tribus regni statibus apud Edinburgh, omnes comites, nobiles, et barones, ac liberi-tenentes dicti regni, venientes ad Castrum de Edinburgh.ʼ From that memorable date may possibly have originated the tradition which survived when, in the middle of last century, Maitland described the hall as ʻa large ancient edifice, formerly the Parliament House, now converted into a barrack.ʼ As to the Tolbooth, the one we know of was only erected in the reign of James V., and while it was building the council met in the Holy Blood aisle of St. Giles's Church.ʼʼ

This and much more, in response to the welcome letter from beyond the sea, was all fully set forth; for the subject gave occasion for frequent correspondence between us, as one in which his sympathies were largely enlisted, and which engaged his latest thoughts; and so it claims a place here. But the letter was never to meet the eye of him for whom it had been penned. His keen appreciation of the humorous aspect that lurks at times in the gravest proceedings was very familiar to his friends, and a touching illustration of it claims notice now. Much that has transpired since his death shows how fully he realized the uncertainty of life, and the fact that the days of his years had already reached man's allotted span. Of this the ample provision in his will for the completion of the works he had undertaken for his native city furnishes the best proof. But on one of his visits to the Castle, in company with friends interested in the progress of the work there, a university professor who was of the party, after satisfying himself as to the extent and character of the designed restorations, proposed a vote of thanks to Mr. Nelson. The proceeding itself was one peculiarly distasteful to him; but in the course of some eulogistic remarks the professor somewhat inopportunely expressed a hope that Mr. Nelson would be spared to see the completion of his costly and patriotic undertaking. As the work was already so far advanced that the finishing of it was a matter of months only, he dryly replied that the learned professor must surely mean to assign him a very brief term of life, for he hoped to see the work finished before the year was out; and as for the cost, he believed it would prove one of the best investments he had ever made. If the lasting appreciation of a generous, public-spirited act furnishes an adequate compensation for such liberality, it was indeed so. But the ominous remark was all too apt. Within three months of that memorable gathering, the words were recalled by some of those who had been present, as they bent in sorrow over his grave.

One of the noticeable gifts of William Nelson was a memory of rare compass and accuracy. An incident distinctly recalled by him in recent years was proved by its association with the death of an aunt to date at a period when he was only two and a half years old. His recollections of playmates went back to early childhood; and he seemed to retain in well-defined and even minute detail events associated with many schoolmates and fellow-students of later years. Numerous as they were, the tie of such early fellowship was never slighted. There was only one point in which his memory failed. A wrong done to himself retained no place in his thoughts; nor did he allow the failures due to misconduct to dull his ear to the appeal of the needy for help. The number of such that made claim to his charity was large. But of friendship in its true sense his conception was high. Of those who were admitted to that intimate relationship he seemed to hold in memory the minutest incidents of a life-long intercourse, and startled them at times by the accuracy with which he recalled the events of long-forgotten years. His large-heartedness was such that he seemed to identify himself with every interest of theirs, with a rare tenderness, as of a love "passing the love of women." One on whom an intimate knowledge of the enduring sacredness of one of his earliest friendships had made a strong impression, thus wrote to me shortly after his death: "The friendship uniting you seemed to me one of the charming things so rarely met in life. That two men with wives and families, business cares, and different pursuits and tastes, should so cleave to one another from early youth onward was refreshing to realize. I always delight in such friendships being possible. They seem the gems shining out from the dull mass of common humanity."

There is no exaggeration here, for the subject of this memoir was of a rare type of humanity; though, if those who most resemble him in all other respects are marked by a like sensitive shrinking from publicity, we may indulge in the pleasant belief that they are more numerous than the world imagines. But it is vain to linger over such fancies. The memory so prompt in business, so retentive in its literary reminiscences, and so responsive to all the sympathetic impulses of love and friendship, suddenly failed. At the very time when his long-desired visit to the classic scenes of Greece was to have been carried out, and every arrangement was completed for the journey, he seemed to lose his hold on the past. The vessel had been determined upon, and the day of departure fixed, when symptoms, little heeded at first, developed into the fatal malady which brought all his plans to a close. The silver cord was loosed. He had finished his course; and on the 10th of September 1887, the very day on which he was to have set out for Greece, he passed from the circle that for so many happy years had been gladdened with the sunshine of his presence, to join the loved ones who had gone before him to the heavenly home. He was one whose creed found its full expression in deeds, not in words. Only in rare moments of confidence did he give utterance to his simple faith. At best the highest efforts of the biographer but dimly approximate to the original. God sends many a beautiful soul into this world to do its appointed work, and then to live only in the memories of the loved ones left behind. Perhaps in this case also it had been better if no biography had been attempted; but he seems to me to have realized in his life that "pure religion" which the apostle James had in view: "To visit the fatherless and the widows in their affliction, and to keep himself unspotted from the world."

The wide-spread manifestations of grief when the news of William Nelson's death became known abundantly manifested the sense of a great public loss. At the urgent request of the city authorities the desire of the family for a strictly private funeral was abandoned. The Lord Provost and magistrates of Edinburgh and the Provost and magistrates of Kinghorn attended in their robes; and along with them the Principal and many of the professors of the University, the President and members of the Royal Scottish Academy, with leading citizens, clergymen, and others, many of whom came from great distances to mark their respect for one whose loss was so widely deplored. The shops were closed as the mournful procession, headed by the employés from Parkside, moved on to the Grange Cemetery, where his remains were laid beside those of his loved father and mother and his brother John, with the graves of Dr. Chalmers and Hugh Miller near by. The turf was fragrant with the wreaths of flowers laid there by many sincere mourners; and it continued to be visited from day to day by crowds, including many humble admirers who deplored the loss of their benefactor, until the turf around was trodden out and had to be replaced. Now that his remains are laid at rest in the quiet cemetery among those of loved ones who formed the happy home circle of his early years, and the busy outer world has resumed its wonted avocations, his widow has erected a memorial tablet to mark the sacred spot, aptly inscribed with the text: "After he had served his generation by the will of God, he fell asleep."

THE END.